BOOK 1

HUNTER THOMAS
AND THE
SMELLY OLD SHOE

Happy Reading!

BY M.V. SOYARS

ILLUSTRATIONS BY CAROLINE HADILAKSONO

Soyars, Megan
Published by Lulu.com
Edited by Emily Coleman
Humor /Fantasy /Children's Series

ISBN-13 978-1492264026

*To my grandmother, Veronica Soyars,
for first implanting in me a love of writing; and
to my grandfather, Bobby Roth, for supporting
me the rest of the way.*

Chapters

CHAPTER ONE

A BALEFUL ATMOSPHERE

Although it took its time getting here, the last day of school has finally arrived at the clean, friendly little town of Abottsville, New Hampshire. My sister Lorraine and I have both lived in Abottsville since we were born, with our mom and dad.

My sister's a year older than I am, but a lot of people mistake us for twins. I'm not *too* insulted by this. After all, Lorraine and I both have the same brown curly hair, blue eyes, and pointed noses. I like Lorraine well enough, and we get along okay considering we're siblings. Lorraine is very daring and adventurous, and she's always thinking up what my father calls "fanciful and irresponsible" ideas.

I'm not close to being like that. I'd rather read a book. Lorraine likes reading too, actually. She's just finished reading *The Chronicles of Narnia* series by C.S. Lewis. For the past two weeks, Lorraine has been talking like an English lady, as well as prefacing every sentence with "oh." This is a somewhat annoying habit, but I'm trying not to complain too much.

Since today was the last day of school, Lorraine and I had decided to take the long, leisurely walk home. Moseying down the cracked sidewalk of Tuttle Street, we'd been gazing at all the inviting stores and restaurants along the way. We usually rode the bus home, but today had such a warm and content feel to it that we'd wanted to walk. Little did I know this feeling wouldn't last for long.

"Oh, look at that!" Lorraine says suddenly to me in her newly acquired British accent.

"What?" I ask.

"There!" She points, and I follow her finger. Across the street is the familiar A&P Grocery and Half-Price Books. But squished between the two stores is a shop that looks quite out of place in our clean neighborhood. It's small and shabby-looking, with a sagging roof, painted red. It looks like one of those physic's shops where you go to have your palm read or look in a crystal ball.

I could swear I'd never seen this shop before, but I remind myself I haven't walked down Tuttle Street in awhile. After all, stores don't just pop up out of nowhere.

"What about it?" I ask Lorraine warily. It looks like she is getting one of her crazy ideas.

"Wouldn't you like to take a look inside?" she says.

"Not particularly."

"Oh, don't be so dry. It looks so queer and interesting. I bet there are a lot of knickknacks inside."

"Who cares? Who likes knickknacks?"

Usually I'm not so reluctant to try something out with Lorraine, but I am today. First of all, this is the first day of summer, and I don't want to spend it in a dusty antique shop. Secondly, the place gives me a creepy feeling, even though it's in the middle of the afternoon and I'm standing across the street.

"*I* like knickknacks," she says. "Besides, Daddy's birthday is coming up and I want to buy him something special."

"Dad doesn't like old things," I answer. Lorraine gives me a look.

"*What*?" I say.

"You're so dry it's not even funny, Hunter. I think I'm going to check it out. You can stay over here on the other side of the street like a good boy and I'll come get you when I'm done."

11

"I'll come," I grumble, feeling myself flush. Lorraine is always complaining about me being a baby.

We cross the street and in a minute are standing on the cracked sidewalk in front of the store. The ominous feeling I got from the place increases. It looks even more ramshackle up close. A rotting, wooden porch surrounds the place. There are a few tiny windows, but you can't see through them; ancient-looking maps have been propped up against the glass from the inside. A sign on the door, scrawled in red paint, gives the shop a name: Monty's.

"Are you still sure you want to go inside?" I ask Lorraine uncertainly.

"Of course," she answers loftily. We climb the porch steps and open the tiny door with a schreeeech....

Lorraine goes in first and I come in after, looking around. It's like entering another world from the brightness of the street. Just like I imagined, it's dark and musty. There are a bunch of old globes and maps around; solemn portraits of people that look like they come from the Victorian Age hang on the walls. Stuffed bookcases teeter everywhere, creating a labyrinth in the tiny room. There are several shelves along one wall, where artifacts have been messily stashed.

On the other side of the room is a desk or counter of some sort, covered with papers and paperweights. An ancient cash register has been set on the desk. Behind it stands a little man with gleaming eyes and a black goatee.

Maybe it's the atmosphere of the shop, or maybe it's my wild imagination, but I don't like the way the man is looking at us.

But Lorraine jerks my attention away by exclaiming, "Oh, come over here and look at this, Hunter!"

She drags me over to the shelves full of antiques. There are all sorts of things on the shelf—old rocks, chipped vases, even rubber-band balls. Lorraine is picking up some sort of gold emblem shaped like two interwoven snakes. I notice that the first snake is eating the second snake's tail.

"Ooh, isn't that grotesque?" she says happily.

Just then, I see an old, worn shoe on the shelf. Picking up the shoe by its broken laces, I say in disgust, "Now who'd want this smelly old shoe?"

"Not just *any* smelly old shoe, young man," says a voice behind me. I spin around; even Lorraine jumps a little. The man from the counter has come up behind us without making any noise. He is smiling, but I don't like the sinister look of it.

"What do you mean?" Lorraine asks curiously over my shoulder.

"What I mean," the man replies delicately, taking the shoe from my hand, "is that this is no ordinary object." His voice carries a slight accent, but I can't place it. He's definitely not American, or British.

"*This* is a Teleporter," he continues. "Hold this shoe in your hand and state any location in the world that you

13

would like to go to—and you will be transported immediately there."

The man is staring at us. I can tell he's trying to see whether we believe him or not. I don't, of course. But Lorraine, who is a year my senior, says "Woww..." in awe behind me.

"That's impossible," I snort.

"Nothing is impossible," the man replies, then looks away from me, as if out of politeness. "Perhaps, to the narrow-minded young gentleman, the world is a place full of restrictions and realities. But to the believer..." he looks past my shoulder to Lorraine, "anything is possible."

I would have snickered at the absurdity of it all, but I don't like the man's glittering eyes or the way he is showing his sharp teeth. I glance at his nametag. It reads A.T. Briner, which is strange, because the name of the shop is Monty's.

"I would so like to buy it," Lorraine says in her best English accent. "How much is it?"

"Twenty-three dollars," the man answers.

"Oh, I only have twenty," Lorraine says regretfully. "I've been saving for Daddy's birthday present, but..." She looks towards me. "Hunter, how much do you have?"

I want to say I have nothing, but the man's penetrating gaze makes me feel like he'd know I was lying. So I reluctantly take out two dollars and eighty-five cents, which is what was left over from my lunch money.

"Close enough, isn't it?" Lorraine asks uncertainly. "Is that twenty-three with or without tax?"

I have a feeling that it was without tax, but the man, who is looking eager, says, "With."

"We're only a few cents off," Lorraine says. "Can we purchase it?"

"I can see how much you want the shoe, young lady, and who am I to deny it to you—over a mere fifteen cents?" the man says. "Certainly you may purchase it."

He starts over towards the counter and we follow him. He rings up our item and takes the twenty-two dollars and eighty-five cents from Lorraine's hand. The man watches us carefully as he places the money in the cash register. As my coins plink, plink, plink in the drawer, they make a foreboding sound.

"Very well!" says A.T. Briner as he hands us the shoe. "Prepare yourselves, for many things await you. Remember, the believer is the seer, and only you can create your own boundaries.

"Good day!" he calls to our backs as we leave. In a minute we are out on the street, blinking in the bright light.

"What a loony!" I say as soon as we are far enough away. It's hard to shake the creepy feeling I got from the man and the shop. It clings to me like a chill.

"He might have been a little deranged-looking," Lorraine admits, "but think, a Teleporter!"

"Aw, come off it," I sneer. "You really don't believe that load, do you?"

"Maybe I do." Lorraine sounds like a lofty English woman. "What's the harm in that?"

"There's plenty of harm in it. It means you're twice as loony as he is—"

"Oh, don't be so dry!"

"—and there's no such thing as magic."

Lorraine shoots me a quick look. For some reason, her look makes me feel stupid and ashamed; I start walking with my hands in my pockets.

"Alright," Lorraine says finally. "Maybe there is no such thing as magic. But it makes me feel so light and free! Like when I'm reading a good adventure story."

"Lorraine, you're twelve years old," I say. "It's time to face reality."

"But it felt so real! Standing there in that shop! When the shoe was in my hand, I felt some sort of power from it. Oh, maybe it's possible; there's no harm in trying it."

I shiver a little, which is strange, but then I remember the feeling I got simply by looking at Monty's from across the street. Something hadn't been right about it. But I definitely didn't remember sensing "power" when I had picked up the shoe. Looking sideways at Lorraine, I say, "I didn't feel anything."

16

Lorraine shrugs and grins. "Oh, probably that 'baseless imagination' running away with me again," she says, quoting Dad.

"You're not going to try it, are you?" I ask. "You know you'll feel pretty dumb when it doesn't work." She looks at me, then laughs.

"Oh, Hunter, you look so worried! The caring younger brother! No, I suppose I won't try it. Just so you'll stop looking so worried."

"You really won't?" I feel slightly reassured.

"I promise."

"Then what are you going to do with the old shoe?" I ask, glancing at it. "Return it to the shop? We could get our money back."

"Maybe," she answers. By now, we've already turned off Tuttle Street and are walking down Worchester Drive, where we live. Worchester is a nice neighborhood with spacey, one-story brick houses, big yards, and shady oak trees. I'm relieved that we're almost home. I feel safe in a familiar place.

"Oh, and don't tell Mom and Daddy about this," Lorraine warns me. "I'll be in trouble if they hear about this newest escapade. I was supposed to save that money for Daddy's present." Now she sounds like she's back on earth, worrying about sane things again.

"Don't worry," I answer. I wonder why I had been scared at the thought of Lorraine using the shoe. Maybe it

the baleful atmosphere of Monty's. Or maybe it
. been that the shoe might actually work, might actually
whisk Lorraine away from me to places unknown. *No, of course not, that's loony,* I think, shaking my head. But there isn't time to dwell on it anymore, because Lorraine and I are climbing up the steps of 318 Worchester Drive, and are home.

CHAPTER TWO

THE SHOE STEALER

The next morning is June 1st. Waking up, I turn over in bed to flip over my calendar to June. My calendar models classic cars, and this month it's a 1970 Ford Mustang. As I roll back over, I try to remember the dream I'd had last night. It had been a foreboding dream; almost a nightmare.

Then I remember the shoe. Had *that* been a dream? I shake my head, trying to throw the last threads of sleep off. No, the shoe had been real. Now fully awake, I sit up and get dressed. Since it's summer, I'd been sleeping in my underwear, so now I put on my pajamas. Lorraine makes fun of me because my pajamas are forest green and have flying pink elephants on them. I don't have any others to wear; Grandma bought me these. Besides, I don't care.

I go into the kitchen, where Lorraine is at the table eating a snickers bar and drinking a coke. From this, I conclude Mom and Dad have already left the house. Grinning, I say to her, "The first day of freedom! What are you going to do today?"

Just then, I notice Lorraine has a funny look on her face. She looks me straight in the eye and says all too casually, "Oh, I thought I'd go over to my friend Mary's today."

"But I thought you'd said Mary got out of school early to go to South Carolina to see her aunt," I reply smugly.

Lorraine thinks if you look someone directly in the eye and speak easily, no one will suspect you are lying. My sister played the part too well, however. "Oh, yeah," she says, blushing and temporarily losing her accent, "I forgot."

A sudden realization strikes me. "You're going to use that shoe, aren't you?" I was sure she was going to try the dang thing as soon as I left the house.

"Oh, Hunter," she says in a regretful voice, "you looked so worried yesterday I said I wouldn't just so you'd feel better."

"You haven't tried it yet, have you?" I snap. "I should have known."

"Oh, shut up, Hunter. You're as dry as an old librarian."

"I bet you're going to try it out right this minute," I say.

"And what's wrong with that? Afraid it might actually work and you'll be proved wrong?"

Lorraine is smirking, so I say, "I just got a bad feeling about that place. Something dark."

"First you're being dry and now you're being melodramatic," she says. "Go play with your friends, Hunter."

"*You* go play with *your* friends."

"I wish I could go see Mary, but she's gone. Mary was the only girl who liked the things I did. Everyone else thinks I'm a 'flighty daydreamer.'"

"Is that what Dad calls you?" I ask.

"No, that's what Alexandra Wilbert calls me," Lorraine says. "Some girl from school."

I sit down, knowing that our argument is over. For awhile, we shut up, then I say hesitantly, "So are you going to try that dumb shoe?"

"Yes, I am," she declares, and I know I'm defeated.

"Can I deter you by saying it looks dangerous?" I say. "If you believe in good magic, you should believe in bad magic."

"Oh, it's just a shoe."

"I didn't like the look of that A.T. Briner. You saw him too, didn't you?" I ask.

"Who?"

21

"The man behind the counter; he snuck up on us and scared me out of my shoes—"

"Oh, him," Lorraine interrupts. "Don't be so rabbity. He was harmless."

"That's not the impression I got."

"Oh, hush." Lorraine gets up to throw away her candy bar wrapper and soda can. "I'm going to try it. Just think of it! A Teleporter! We could be taken anywhere we wanted. Think of the sights we could see! It's what people dream of, Hunter. It's almost like a time machine."

"Yeah, sure," I say sarcastically.

"Oh, fine," she says. "You can sit here like a toad and have no interesting happenings in your life for all I care." Then she turns around and goes to her room.

I sit by myself for awhile in the kitchen. Yesterday, Lorraine had given me a similar challenge, then I found myself standing in front of Monty's. Would I make the same mistake today? I can hear Lorraine messing around in her room, probably getting the shoe ready. Abruptly, I start up from my chair and rush to her room. I stop in the doorway and watch her get the shoe from the top of the closet. When she turns around and sees me, she grins as if she knew I would come.

"So where are you planning to teleport yourself?" I ask, crossing my arms across my chest and trying to sound gruff.

22

"I thought this would be a test run," Lorraine answers. "I'll just go a short distance since this is my first time." She points out the open window. "I'll try to Teleport myself from this room to the backyard. You can watch and see if I appear."

I crazily wonder if I should grab the shoe from her hand and run. *Aw, come on, Hunter,* I reprimand myself. *The shoe won't work. There's no such thing as black magic any more than there is a thing as good magic. Let Lorraine try it and make a fool of herself when it doesn't work.*

But a kid has an easier time believing in closet monsters than the Tooth Fairy at night, even when he knows both aren't real. Plus, I'm a pessimist by nature. What if the shoe works, but whisks her away somewhere—dangerous? Meanwhile, Lorraine is watching me get bleaker and bleaker with my arms crossed.

"Well, will you?" she demands.

"Will I what?"

"Watch through the window to see if I Teleport into the backyard. Honestly, what's wrong with you, Hunter? You act like you've been ordered to watch me walk the plank. Sometimes you're dry and sometimes you're melodramatic, always at the wrong time. You're supposed to be excited! Oh, imagine if it could work!" Lorraine is laughing and her eyes are bright. "Watch me, will you? Here we go!"

I open my mouth to object, to say why can't we just try it on the neighbor's cat, but the words won't come out— it's too late—

"I want to go to my backyard!" Lorraine squeals with her eyes squeezed tight like she's about to receive a surprise present....

But nothing happens.

My arms have dropped, but I cross them again, smirking. *See, I told you so*, I'm about to say, but then there's a sudden gust of wind. I see Lorraine in the center of the room, spinning around and around like a top. I try to shout out, but the wind tears my voice away, becoming so strong and fast that I fly out of the room and bang into the hallway wall. Squinting, I see Lorraine still spinning in the room, but she's getting smaller; the color of her brown hair, red shirt, and blue jeans melding together like paint—then she is gone.

The wind stops and it's still and silent as death, like after a tornado. For a moment, I think I'm going to faint. But then I hear a shout from outside. I scramble to my feet, burst into Lorraine's room, and hoist myself out of the open window into the backyard. Lorraine is standing on the grass, looking woozy, her hair all over her face from the wind. I'm about to run to her and hug her, thankful that she's alive. But just before I can, I hear another voice.

It's coming from our neighbor's backyard. Mrs. Esther Hazelton is staring at us on the other side of the chain-link fence. She has a pair of hedge clippers in her hands; it looks like she's just been trimming her mountain laurel bushes. I gulp. She's staring at us like we just popped out of the ground, which, in essence, is just what Lorraine did.

"Where did you come from?" Mrs. Hazelton asks hesitantly, as if she might be afraid of the answer.

"Ah, I just came out of the window," I say.

"And—and what about Lorraine?"

"Oh, I came through the window, too, ma'am," Lorraine answers, with that 'I'm lying' look on her face. I also notice that she has lost her British accent.

"Well then," Mrs. Hazelton says, rubbing her face and looking embarrassed and confused. "Just shows you how senile I'm getting in my old age, ha-ha." She forces a laugh, turning away from us. We, as if in a dream, walk back to the window and crawl inside. As soon as we are safely back in Lorraine's room, I throw my arms around her.

"Oh, let go, you're breaking my ribs, Hunter," she giggles. I let go, feeling dumb.

"Just glad you're safe," I say gruffly. Now it's Lorraine's turn to grab me and break my ribs. "It worked, it worked!" she cries. "That smelly old shoe! As soon as I saw it in Monty's, I knew it! I just knew it was that sort of place!

Think of where we'll go now! There's no end to the possibilities!"

We dance around for a moment, as crazy as monkeys. Now I know how it feels to have your heart burst; burst into a million pieces, showering you with wealth like dollar bills.

"Let's go somewhere now!" I yelp. "And when we get tired of traveling, we can sell that dang shoe for a million bucks!"

"Where is the shoe?" she asks, still laughing. We both look around for a minute, but don't see it anywhere. Somewhat vaguely and stupidly, I check my pockets. I'm still a little dazed from our recent occurrence. But Lorraine is becoming serious and worried as she checks under the bed. Straightening, she exclaims, "Oh, I left it outside!" and looks relieved.

I don't feel relieved, though, and that old portent feeling is starting to come back over me as I turn to the window. A movement in the backyard makes me freeze. I see our neighbor, Mrs. Hazelton, exiting our yard from a little gate at the back fence, which leads into the alley. Then I watch her go into her yard.

She is holding something in her hand.

CHAPTER THREE

INTO THE LIONS' DEN

I gulp. Lorraine comes to the window.

"What is it? Oh, damn it!" she curses, sounding like a horrified English woman. "She didn't have a shoe in her hand, did she?"

"She had something."

Lorraine pushes me out of the way and boosts herself out the window. Jumping into the yard, she calls out, "Oh, Mrs. Hazelton!" but it's too late. Mrs. Hazelton's back door slams, and I know she has gone inside. I climb out of the window and stand by Lorraine, who is stock still. My legs feel weak, and I realize I am tense with dread for some reason.

"Oh, that's it," Lorraine says grimly. "Someone will have to go inside and ask Mrs. Hazelton for the shoe."

"Won't Mrs. Hazelton think it's funny some kid is asking for a smelly old shoe back?" I ask.

"Well, wasn't it a little funny of her to come into our yard and take the shoe?" Lorraine snaps. I can't help but wonder if Mrs. Hazelton knows the real power and purpose of the Teleporter. That would be more than enough reason to take it.

"I had a bad feeling about this shoe business from the beginning," I say. Lorraine gives me a disgusted look.

"Oh, stop being so melodramatic. Just go over there, ring the doorbell and ask for it."

"*I'm* not going over there," I declare. "Besides, I'm in my pajamas."

"So what? It's not just a shoe, it's a Teleporter!"

"If you want it so bad, you go over there!"

"Well, if you're going to be so rabbity, I will!" she snaps. "Since when have you cared you wear pink elephant pajamas! You act like I'm sending you over to spend an hour with her and the Knitting Society! You're just getting the Teleporter back! I would have thought you wanted it back."

Muttering to herself, Lorraine storms towards the gate that leads to our front yard. I *do* want the Teleporter back, but I can't erase the bad feeling I have about Mrs. Hazelton. Nevertheless, I follow Lorraine, shutting the gate behind us. As we cross the front yard, Lorraine starts to quiet down. Thankfully, she never stays angry for long.

As we enter the Hazelton's yard, she says, "I'm sure Mrs. Hazelton will give it back. She's a very nice lady. What would she want with an old shoe, anyway?" But Lorraine's voice is too casual, and I know she's thinking what I'm thinking—what if Mrs. Hazelton knows what the "shoe" really is?

Like our porch, Mrs. Hazelton's porch is wide and wooden, but hers is covered with pink and purple potted flowers. She also has a porch swing. The swing looks stiff and uncomfortable, however, and a few more potted flowers are set on it, so you couldn't sit down if you wanted to.

Lorraine rings the doorbell of the house, and we stand waiting by the flowers, listening to the bell chime. We wait for several moments, but there is silence in the house. I become aware of the sounds of sparrows singing on our street. Their cheerful tones seem to mock us as we stand stupid and expectant on Mrs. Hazelton's porch. By now, a cold dread has crept over me. I feel as if I'm standing in front of Monty's on Tuttle Street. I shift and say, "Should we try it again?"

"Well, Mrs. Hazelton is slow and it would be rude, but..." she says, then rings the doorbell. We listen to it chime again through the house.

"Oh, I know she's inside and she's not deaf," Lorraine says angrily. "And I know the doorbell works."

"She knows it's us," I say solemnly.

"Then she should answer it, shouldn't she?"

"Maybe she knows what the Shoe really is," I reply.

"How would she know that? Do you think she went into Monty's before us?"

"I doubt it," I answer. "We left the window open, remember?"

"What window?"

"The window to your room!" I say. "We were blabbing about the shoe in there, remember? Then you Teleported. Mrs. Hazelton must have put two and two together."

"Do you really think so?" Lorraine turns away from me to stare at the stubbornly closed door. "So do you think she's already Teleported, then?"

"Maybe."

"Well, there's only one way to find out," she declares. She's gotten that look I'm beginning to dread.

"How's that?" I ask, even though I don't really want the answer.

"Oh, there you go, sounding dry again," Lorraine says. "Dry as a calculus professor."

"Was I being dry? Do I sound dry?" I say to the swinging flower pots.

"Oh hush," she says. "You characteristically sound dry whenever I bring up an idea. I was simply suggesting going around to the backyard and knocking on her screen door."

So we jump over Mrs. Hazelton's fence and enter the yard, which is a lot bigger than ours. Mountain laurel bushes surround the whole place. In the middle of this, there is a large patio with a quaint-looking rose garden in front of it. Normally, I would be enjoying this scenery, but there are more important things at hand.

"Come on," Lorraine hisses, dragging me over to the screen door of the Hazelton's sunroom. By pressing our noses against the screen, we can faintly see the inside of a dark house. Lorraine steps back and calls in her best British accent, "Oh, Mrs. Hazelton!" No answer. Lorraine begins to ring her hands.

"Maybe she went out the front door when we came around back here," I say.

"Maybe," she replies faintly. She tries to push open the screen door in a half-hearted way, not really expecting it to open. But to our surprise, it slides open a few inches. My heart jumps into my throat, and we turn our heads to stare at each other. Then I scan the yard and alley to see if anyone is watching. o one. I prod Lorraine and hiss, "Open it all the way!"

She tugs it open and we both leap inside the sunroom. Cool, musty air from a fan hits us. Lorraine shuts the screen door behind us. There is another screen door in front of us, leading into the rest of the house. We approach it cautiously. The house beyond looks dark and empty. My heart is pounding, and I feel like I'm trespassing into a lions'

31

den. Besides, my conscience is bothering me. I know it's unethical (as well as against the law) to break into a home. But after all, Mrs. Hazelton has stolen our Shoe. And it hadn't been just any Shoe; it had been a Teleporter.

I glance at Lorraine. She licks her lips, looking serious. The usual exuberant, adventurous look on her face is gone. As we try the next door, it slides open easily. A feeling of impending doom descends upon me. I feel myself sweating and shaking, and wish I didn't wimp out so easily. Lorraine, alert but satisfied, gives me the 'okay' sign. I don't feel 'okay' though.

The house is quiet, too quiet, like when someone is holding their breath to watch you. I flinch when Lorraine says, "Oh, stop acting like you're walking on pins, Hunter. No one's in here but us."

"Do you think the Shoe is in here?" I ask.

"I doubt it," she answers. "Mrs. Hazelton has probably already left to the Bahamas with it or something."

"She must have took Mr. Hazelton with her, too," I say.

"Well, let's look around to see if the Shoe's here, just in case," Lorraine says, moving into the kitchen. I feel anxious to leave. I wonder if I should follow Lorraine or split off and look in another room. If I go off and look by myself, the search will be over faster, but I feel uncomfortable without Lorraine.

As I stand thinking, there is a sudden noise behind me; the rush of an attack. But before I can turn around, someone is pinning my arms to my side and shouting, "I got you, you little bandit!"

I scream, and am spun around to face my captor. For some reason, I expect to see A.T. Briner's face leering down at me, but it's only Mr. Hazelton. Mr. Hazelton, of course, is Mrs. Hazelton's husband. Mr. Hazelton is a retired college football player and coach, and is still as strong and limber now as he was in his prime. As he shakes me, I fight the urge to weep for mercy and choke, "Mr. Hazelton! It's me, Hunter Thomas!"

Mr. Hazelton stops shaking me. "Hunter, from next door?"

"Yes, sir!"

Just then, Mr. Hazelton looks over my shoulder, so I know Lorraine has entered into the scene.

"What are you two brats doing here?" Mr. Hazelton snarls. "Don't you know you're breaking and entering?" I've never liked Mr. Hazelton much. He doesn't have a very approachable personality, which isn't good for a large man.

"Umm," Lorraine says.

"Please, sir," I squeak, interrupting her, "if maybe you could let me go, I could explain."

Mr. Hazelton glares at me through beady eyes, but releases me. I straighten up and adjust my collar, feeling vulnerable in my pajamas. "The thing is—" I start to say, then stop. What is the 'thing'? Everyone is staring at me, including the photos on the wall of Mr. Hazelton when he was a star center.

"Welll...?" says Mr. Hazelton.

I gulp and shake my head, unable to continue. I want to ask where Mrs. Hazelton is, but I think I already know the answer.

Curling his lip in disgust, Mr. Hazleton says, "Well, it looks like I'm going to have to call the police on you little folks." He points to the couch, and with no other option, Lorraine and I sink down on it. "You two sit here. Don't even think of going anywhere." Then he turns on his heel and marches into the kitchen.

Feeling dizzy, I put my head down in my hands. I hear Mr. Hazelton muttering on the phone in the kitchen. "Yes, the next-door kids...just standing around, the boy was...the girl came in later...How should I know? Let me ask them...Hey!" Mr. Hazelton calls out to us, "are your parents home?"

"No," Lorraine answers in a steady voice. Inexplicably, the way you sometimes do after a traumatizing experience, I start to laugh. The whole situation is pretty hilarious. A day ago, if someone had told me I would soon be breaking into the Hazelton's home to steal back a smelly old shoe that could Teleport you anywhere on the planet in a second, I would have told them they were crazy.

34

Meanwhile, Mr. Hazelton has hung up on the police and entered the living room, whereupon he says, "I don't see anything funny, but the cops will be here any minute, and then we'll contact your parents."

Immediately, I stop laughing. Lorraine puts her arm around my shoulders. We wait for almost an eternity together on the couch. Mr. Hazelton stands over us, his arms crossed, daring us to shift or cough. A couple times, Lorraine opens her mouth to speak, but the glare Mr. Hazelton shoots us makes her fall silent. Just then, I hear a vehicle pull up. We all glance out the window to see who it is. I'm expecting a patrol car, but I see something worse. Mom's red Honda is pulling into our driveway.

CHAPTER FOUR

ABOTTSVILLE'S LOCAL LAW ENFORCEMENT

I gulp. Mr. Hazelton grins.

"That wouldn't be Mrs. Thomas, would it?" he asks.

When Lorraine nods, he says, "Well, why don't we go out to meet her?"

With a hand on each of our shoulders, Mr. Hazelton steers us gleefully outside into his front yard and over to Mom, who is getting out of the car. When she looks up, she starts to say politely, "Hello, Marty," then stops. I suppose a pretty strange scene is meeting her eyes. Mr. Hazelton is practically dragging us towards her, smiling in a way that is very rare for him. Lorraine and I must be looking frightened and wan; I know I'm about to pee in my pants. Plus, I'm still in my bare feet and wearing pink elephant pajamas.

Now Mr. Hazelton is standing face to face with Mom, looking triumphant.

"Well," he says. "These are your kids, aren't they?"

"Yes," my mother answers, looking as though she regrets it.

"*I* just caught them breaking into my house."

"What?!" My mother grips her purse. "What were they doing in there?"

"Sneaking around. I overheard them talking like they were looking for a shoe or something. Do you know anything about that?"

I think I flinch. Mom says, "No, I can't imagine—"

At that moment, we hear a patrol car pull up. We all turn our heads to see it coast almost boredly into the Hazelton's driveway. Two cops get out, stretching and adjusting their belts. They look tough and tired. *They must get a lot of calls about kids trespassing into other people's homes*, I think, *they must figure this is all routine.*

They're both typical members of the police squad. One is fat with a mustache, and the other is young and blond; a rookie, maybe. The two come over, and the fat cop says, "You Mr. Hazelton, sir?" I read his tag; it says 'Meyers.'

"Yep," Mr. Hazelton says. He gives me and Lorraine a little shake. "These are the two kids that broke in."

37

"Please," Lorraine says to Officer Meyers in her best British accent, "could you tell Mr. Hazelton to let go of us?"

"Let 'em go, sir," Meyers says seriously, and we are released. Then Meyers grins at my sister and adds, "A little English lady, are you?"

Lorraine straightens up, looking haughty, but I break in. "No sir, she just pretends. Her accent is fake."

Lorraine shoots me a glare, but Meyers just looks towards Mom and grins again.

"Mighty cute kids you've got there. You're Mrs. Thomas, I'm guessing?"

Mom, who seems to be rather dazed with all this, just nods. Then Officer Meyers takes out a yellow notepad and a pen. The second officer, Wilson, shifts to his other foot and puts a hand on his holster.

"So," Officer Meyers says, "can you clarify exactly what happened?" He squints up at Marty.

"Well, I was sleeping in the bedroom when I heard the sunroom door out back open—"

"Why don't we go over and look at the scene of the crime?" Officer Meyers suggests, so we all troop over and soon are standing in the Hazelton's backyard, staring dumbly at the sunroom screen door.

"Anyway," Mr. Hazelton continues, "I heard this door open, and as you can see, it is open..." Now we walk into the sunroom and stare at the second door. "Then I hear this one open, so I get up to see who it is..." Now we go into the living room. Mr. Hazelton points to the right, where we can see the doorway of the master bedroom.

"I go to my doorway and see these two kids just come on in like they own the place. They talk like they're looking for some kind of shoe. Then the girl goes into the kitchen. I jump out into the living room and scare the boy. Then he tells me that they are the Thomas kids from next door. So I call you men up and that's the story."

Now it's time for Officer Meyers to ask questions. His first question is, "What time did the children enter the living room?" His voice is sharp.

"Ah, around 10:00," Mr. Hazelton answers.

"Do you have a wife?" is the next question. It's a sudden and unrelated question, so Mr. Hazelton looks momentarily startled.

"Yeah—yes."

"Where was she during this time?"

"She left," Mr. Hazelton answers. "About five minutes before the kids came in, Esther came into my room and said she was going out for awhile."

"So you were alone in the house when the children came in?" Meyers asks.

"That's right," Mr. Hazelton says.

The next question makes me start slightly. "You say they were 'looking for some kind of a shoe.' What does that mean? Is that the reason they broke in?"

"Maybe," he says.

"Then you jumped into the living room and scared the boy. What do you mean?"

"I didn't hurt him or anything. I just grabbed him to keep him from going anywhere, like the girl had."

"Where did the girl go?"

"Into the kitchen. But she came back out when I grabbed the boy."

"Was anything in the home stolen...or disturbed by the children?"

Sudden fear flashes into Mr. Hazelton's eyes. "I didn't check!"

"Well, why don't you right now?" Meyers suggests. Marty leaves to tear around the house for awhile, goes into the kitchen, then comes back out. "Nothing," he says.

Now Meyers turns toward us. "Time to ask the kids a few questions." I gulp, even though the officer is smiling.

"So," he says, "why don't we start with the classic: 'why did you break into the Hazelton home'? Was it to look for a shoe?"

"No," Lorraine answers flatly, looking Officer Meyers dead in the eye. "Hunter and I," she glances over at me, "were talking to Mrs. Hazelton outside around 10:00. Mrs. Hazelton said she was leaving for awhile, and that Hunter and I were free to come inside the house while she was gone, to get a...deck of cards."

"To get a deck of cards," Meyers says skeptically. Officer Wilson, however, smiles benevolently, as though the whole matter has been cleared up by Lorraine's explanation.

"Esther would never give two dirty kids permission to enter my home while she was gone and I was sleeping!" Mr. Hazleton breaks in loudly.

"Excuse me," Mom breaks in, speaking for the first time. "These are *my* children you're speaking about, Marty."

"Now, now, let's all settle down," Meyers says lazily, putting his hand on his holster.

After Mr. Hazelton has managed to calm himself, Meyers clears his throat and addresses him. "So, according to you, your wife never would've given the children permission to enter your home?"

"That's right," Mr. Hazelton huffs.

"Exactly what is the relationship between your wife and the children next door?"

"*We're* fine with them, as long as they keep their snotty noses out of *our* backyard!"

"Excuse *me!*" Mom repeats. She and Lorraine are sharing identical indignant looks.

Meyers breaks in quickly, as if trying to head off confrontation. "I assume you are speaking for your wife as well?"

"Well, no," Mr. Hazelton admits. "*She* likes them well enough."

"Well enough to allow them inside your home?"

41

I hold my breath. Thankfully, Lorraine and I have always gotten along with Mrs. H. (I'm not saying anything about Marty!) But we've never been invited into the house. What would Mr. Hazelton say next?

"No," he snaps. "Not if I'm sleeping oblivious in my bed! Who knows what they could have done unsupervised, trashed the kitchen—"

Officer Meyers interrupts Mr. Hazelton's rant. "Perhaps she *did* tell you the kids were coming over. It's possible you simply didn't hear her. What state where you in when Esther came into the room and said she was leaving? Were you semiconscious?"

"No, I was wide awake. All she said was, 'I'm going to be gone for awhile.'"

"But she couldn't have told you we were coming over!" Lorraine bursts in suddenly.

All eyes turn towards her. My heart jumps in my chest.

"Why in the hell not?" Mr. Hazelton snaps.

"Oh, because," Lorraine explains, "Mrs. Hazelton didn't know *then* that we were coming over."

"See, see!" Marty Hazelton howls, pointing at us. "They admit it. They broke in! Trespassers!"

"No, that's not what I meant!"

"Then what did you mean?" he spits.

Lorraine turns to the officers, fixing them with a guiltless gaze. "Mrs. Hazelton didn't know we were coming in *yet*. She didn't find out until later, after she had already left the house."

"Can you explain that?" Meyers asks seriously.

Lorraine clears her throat quaintly and straightens, clasping her hands in front of her. From long experience, I know these are the prefacing signs to a Lorraine-cock-and-bull story.

"This morning around 10:00 a.m.," she begins, "Hunter and I were playing outside."

'Playing outside'? I grimace. *Where is she going with this?* Meanwhile, Officer Meyers has taken out his yellow notepad and begins to scribble. He nods at Lorraine to continue.

"Just then, Mrs. Hazelton walked by us on the sidewalk. Hunter and I said, 'Hello, Mrs. Hazelton!' 'Hello, Hunter; hello, Lorraine,' she said."

"Then what happened?" Wilson blurts excitedly.

"Well, after we had exchanged pleasantries, we began a bit of polite conversation. Eventually, the subject of playing cards came up. So, I said, 'Mrs. Hazelton, Hunter and I absolutely *love* to play Go Fish.'"

I can't help myself from casting a sidelong glance toward Mom at this one. She still looks pretty dazed. I'm praying she won't announce that Lorraine and I almost *never* play Go Fish.

"—So I said, 'But unfortunately, we've lost our only cards.' So she said, 'How awful. But I actually happen to

43

have a deck of playing cards in the kitchen.' So I said, 'Oh, how wonderful! Could we borrow them?' So she said, 'Certainly. But I'm in a bit of a hurry to get on the bus. Can you and Hunter be trusted to let yourselves in alone to get the cards?' So I said, 'Oh, of course.'" Lorraine falls silent, staring expectantly up at the officers.

"I see," Meyers says, rubbing his chin. Then he turns to Mr. Hazelton. "Does this story sound plausible to you?"

"Humph," he grunts.

"I see. Yet the children entered the house through the back door rather than the front. Why is that?"

"Because," Lorraine explains, "Mrs. Hazelton had already locked the front door. She simply told us to get in through the back door, which as you already know, was open. She also warned us not to wake up her husband, who was sleeping in the bedroom."

"I see," Meyers says for the third time today. "Did you retrieve the cards?"

My knees buckle slightly under me as I hope Mrs. Hazelton actually *owns* a set of playing cards.

"No, we didn't," Lorraine answers. "But I can show the cards to you, if you want."

"What do you mean?"

"Oh, as you know, I went inside the kitchen as soon as I entered the house. I was about to grab the cards off the table when Mr. Hazelton frightened my brother."

44

"I see," Meyers says. "Yet you didn't relate this story to Mr. Hazelton before he called us."

"I wanted to," Lorraine explains loftily, "but I was afraid to say anything. Mr. Hazelton was extremely intimidating."

Meyers' mustache twitches. He's grinning: "Let's see the cards, then."

Our little assembly squeezes through the door into the kitchen. Presently, we are all grouped around the kitchen table, staring down at a worn pack of playing cards sitting in the middle of it. Meyers picks them up and studies them as if to confirm they are real.

"I see," he says for the fifth time.

"That doesn't prove anything!" Mr. Hazelton slavers. "My wife never plays cards. And I didn't hear these dirty kids say *anything* about a deck of cards when they were snooping around. This could be a set up! The cards are a ploy!"

Just as the situation is getting out of hand, Officer Wilson is struck by a sudden inspiration.

"Oh, oh!" he exclaims loudly. "I know how to solve this! Let's call Mrs. Hazelton and ask her what she said!"

"Good thinking, kid." Meyers pats Wilson on the shoulder. "Let's do that." Then he glances at Mr. Hazelton, who says nastily, "Well, if you know where she's at, that's okay with me."

"Well, we don't. We were hoping you did."

"Wherever she is, she'll be back in a few minutes," he grumbles. "Then we can settle everything. Let's just wait out front."

Lorraine and I exchange looks of dread. Our subdued party troops to the front yard, where we stand around and wait on the front porch.

A few awkward moments of silence pass. Then Meyers clears his throat and asks, "So kids, how's your summer going?"

"Fine, sir," Lorraine and I both mumble.

Mr. Hazelton blurts, "I'll go get some sodas." He hurriedly exits the scene.

When he returns with Pepsis in hand, Meyers turns around, adjusting his belt, and says, "Actually, Marty, we're on a time crunch here—" (Wilson looks at his watch) "—and my partner and I have just got to go. As much as we'd like to stay and socialize, we just can't. Call me when you've contacted Esther. Jim Meyers." He shakes Marty's hand, then Mom's. "Ryan Wilson." Wilson shakes their hands.

As the two men step off the porch, Mr. Hazelton yelps, "But what about the kids? They'll try to make a break for it! They won't want to face the consequences!"

Jim Meyers turns back to look at us. He's grinning, trying to suppress a laugh. I smile half-heartedly back, and Lorraine is trying to look like a little English angel.

"I don't think you'll have to worry about them," Meyers says. "They look like honest kids to me." He winks and heads back to the patrol car. The men buckle up, then pull out of the drive. We watch them coast along the street and disappear around a corner. Then I turn to look at Mom. Her face is still a little pale. "Come on, children," she says faintly, putting an arm around each of our shoulders. We go down the steps and then cross the yard to our house.

"You watch those kids of yours!" We hear Marty Hazelton shout behind us. "Don't turn your back on 'em!"

"I won't," Mom replies, without turning her head. And then to us: "You all are going to be in so much trouble when your father gets home..."

I gulp.

CHAPTER FIVE

INTERROGATION

Several hours later, I am to be found lying flat on my back in bed, stuck in my bedroom. Dad has already arrived home, punishments have already been dealt (two weeks' worth of grounding). So here I am, wondering about what to do next. Thoughts are chasing each other like squirrels around in my head. Does Mrs. Hazelton actually have the Shoe? If so, what is she doing with it? Is she going to bring it back?

In the next moment, my bedroom door flies open. I start straight up in bed and give a yell. (Come on, gimme a break. My nerves were already on edge.) But it's only Lorraine.

"Shh!" she hisses at me.

"Sorry," I whisper as my heart slows down. "What are you doing in here?"

"I need to talk to you, of course."

"You're not allowed in here!" I hiss, glancing into the hallway.

"Why in the heavens not?"

"Maybe you didn't get the gist of Dad's rant to us," I explain, "but I did. We're not allowed out of our rooms unless it's to go to the bathroom or something."

Lorraine rolls her eyes in disdain. "Don't be silly, Hunter. We can visit *each other's* rooms. The thing I need to talk to you about is—"

Just then, we both hear a car pull up into the Hazelton's drive outside.

"Oh, no," Lorraine says, sounding like the Queen about to faint. "It's the police. They've already come back."

I clamber out of bed. "Do you think Mrs. Hazelton's come back, too?"

Lorraine snorts. "I doubt it. She's probably in Jamaica or some exotic place—"

I shush her as I move to my window. Fortunately, it looks into the Hazelton's house. I can just make out a patrol car in their driveway. Lorraine comes up behind me and peeks over my shoulder.

"Open it," she whispers. The window is open just a crack. I push it up the rest of the way, feeling nervous. Faintly, we hear the doorbell ring. I can't see what's happening on the front porch, but I hear the door open, and

Marty Hazelton's grouchy voice: "Well, it took you long enough."

"Donut breaks, you know," chimes a voice that might be Officer Ryan Wilson's.

"Ha, ha," Mr. Hazelton says sarcastically.

"You'll have to excuse my partner, Mr. Hazelton," Officer Jim Meyers says. "He has a bad sense of humor. May we come inside?"

"Sure, sure," Mr. Hazelton mutters. The next minute the door slams. Lorraine and I turn to look at each other.

"Mr. Hazelton doesn't sound very happy," I say slowly. Then, even though I already know the answer, I ask, "What do you think that means?"

"It means," Lorraine answers grimly, "Esther Hazelton hasn't returned yet."

"But she has to come back sometime!" I insist. "I mean, she couldn't have just left forever without telling her husband, could she?"

"Oh, who knows?" Lorraine shrugs. "They weren't very happily married, were they? Mr. Hazelton's never had a very nice personality."

Before I can answer, we both hear footsteps out in the hallway. I shove a disgruntled Lorraine into my closet and leap back on the top of my bed, forcing myself to look carelessly at the ceiling.

Just in time, it seems, because Dad appears in the doorway. His face looks more lined than usual, probably due to the fact that he blew his top only hours earlier. Our father hadn't been very happy to learn that his two children had suffered a brush with the law while he was at work. I notice he's still wearing his office clothes.

"Hi, Dad," I say, sitting up on my bed.

"Hi, son," he mumbles, rubbing his neck. "Is Lorraine in here?"

"Of course not," I answer, fighting the guilty urge to look at my closed closet door.

"She better not be," he grumbles. "I don't want you two together, cooking up more schemes to get in trouble with the cops."

"We didn't break in!" I say loudly. Lorraine's 'we just walked in to get a deck of cards' explanation for the misdemeanor seemed to have gone over with the cops, but not with our shrewder father. He smelled something fishy.

"Whatever. I just came in to tell you that the police will be coming over after they've dealt with Marty. They want to interrogate you both, and they'll probably fine *us*."

"They won't fine you," I insist. "We told you Mrs. Hazelton said we could come in. They can't fine you unless they can actually prove we're guilty."

Dad is staring at me. I blink innocently. I don't look it, but sometimes I'm a better liar than Lorraine.

"Alright," he says finally. "Then change out of your pajamas into something nice. You'll want to give the officers a good impression." As he leaves my room, he calls over his shoulder, "And tell Lorraine she can come out of your closet."

Lorraine bounds out, looking excited. "Oh, I think we've got Dad fooled!" she squeals, clasping her hands. "And even if he isn't fooled, he'll act like he is in front of the police. He *wants* to get us off the hook; I mean, who wants to pay a fine?"

"Shh!" I remonstrate at her. "Do you want Dad to overhear us? Now get out of my room; I have to get ready!"

As soon as she springs out, I start dressing. Unlike the always optimistic Lorraine, I feel tense. In a few minutes, local law enforcement will be parked in our living room. Would we be able to hoodwink them into letting us off? I take a last minute toilet break and brush my teeth in front of the mirror. The face that stares back at me looks faintly green. The doorbell rings, and I choke on my toothpaste. Washing out my mouth quickly, I hear my parents down the hall greeting the cops.

"Of course," my father is saying. "I'll call the children—they're in their rooms—Hunter, Lorraine, the police are here!"

No kidding. Swallowing, I step out of the bathroom. Lorraine and I meet in the hallway. She gives me a hearty 'it's okay' sign. I manage to nod weakly. We walk into the living room and are greeted by Officers Meyers and Wilson.

"Hi, kids," Meyers says in a gruff yet friendly voice. Ryan Wilson gives us a jaunty wave.

"Oh, hello," Lorraine replies, curtsying like a little English girl.

"You've got some cute kids, Mr. and Mrs. Thomas," Meyers compliments, grinning. I can't help but stupidly hope that the cops might just let us go because Lorraine is giving them a good impression.

"Thank you," Dad answers as Mom asks, "Would you men like anything to eat or drink, perhaps?"

Officer Wilson opens his mouth eagerly, but Meyers jabs him in the ribs with his elbow and says, "Just coffee would be fine. Two blacks, please."

"I like sugar!" Wilson manages to get out as Mom bustles into the kitchen.

Dad offers the two men seats and they settle onto the couch.

"You all can sit down too, of course," Meyers says, gesturing to Dad, Lorraine, and me. We settle back in the three remaining seats; my stomach feels like a squirming bag of worms. Mom thankfully causes a delay as she bustles in with the coffees and sugar. Another chair is brought in from the kitchen for her, the officers take prefacing sips of coffee, and the interrogation is ready to begin.

"So," Meyers says, looking around at us all, "let's begin by reviewing the facts we have. We'll start with the story correlated by Marty Hazelton. According to him, at roughly 10:00 a.m., a fully dressed Mrs. Hazelton entered the bedroom, and upon waking her husband, told him that she'd be leaving for awhile."

Officer Meyers pauses, as if waiting for this information to sink in. "Around ten minutes later, he heard something of a commotion in the living room. He got up to investigate, caught the boy and girl, then called the police."

Meyers looks grave now. I let my eyes rove around the rest of our little huddle. Dad appears musing, Mom concerned, Lorraine absorbed, and Ryan Wilson expectant. I hope *I* look innocent, even though I still feel a little queasy.

Meyers continues. "He also claims he overheard the two children talking about a shoe of some sort."

"A shoe?!" Lorraine butts in, as if the thought of a shoe is somehow distasteful. As the officers stare at her, she continues extremely carelessly, "What would Hunter and I want with a smelly old *shoe*?"

I fight the urge to groan out loud. Lorraine's overbearing acting is going to ruin it all! Forced to divert the officers' attention away from her, I croak, "Ah, what did Mr. Hazelton say after that?"

"Yes, uhhh..." Meyers has apparently lost his train of thought.

"Well, then he said," Ryan butts in importantly, "that during the *alleged*—" (he forms quotation marks in the air) "—break in, he didn't hear anything about a deck of cards."

"That's right," Meyers says, looking slightly annoyed at being interrupted.

"That doesn't mean anything," Lorraine replies in an airy tone. "He might have interpreted 'cards' for 'shoes.' Isn't it more probable that we were searching for a deck of cards rather than a single shoe?"

"That's all very well," Meyers says, "but we still have a pretty strange case here. The thing is, Mrs. Hazelton hasn't turned up yet."

"She hasn't?" my father asks, looking bewildered.

"'Fraid not," Meyers answers heavily. "According to the facts, she went missing around 10:00 a.m. It's now 7:00 at night. No hide nor hair of her yet."

He fixes me and Lorraine with a beady eye. I sink a little lower in my seat.

"If the kids' story is correct, *you* were the last persons to see her. She told you that see was in a hurry to get on the bus, right?"

"Right," Lorraine answers.

"Which bus she getting on?"

"Umm...the one leaving at 10:00."

"Did she tell you where she was going?"

"No."

"How did she look when you last saw her? Anxious...maybe distraught?"

"No...more preoccupied, I guess." For the first time during the questioning, Lorraine breaks eye contact with Meyers. She glances down at her folded hands before looking back up at him.

"Preoccupied?"

"Oh, like she had something else on her mind. She obviously had somewhere very important to go. If she hadn't, she wouldn't have let us inside the house alone, would she?"

Genius. Pure genius. Her whole story made sense, even to me, and I knew the whole thing was a load of hooey.

"I see," Meyers says characteristically. The old yellow notepad's out again as he jots down facts. Then he glances up at my parents.

"You two wouldn't happen to know anything about Esther Hazelton's disappearance, would you?"

As Dad shakes his head, Mom says in a faint voice, "How strange...Esther gone...and for so long...I wonder why..."

As her voice trails away into space, Lorraine and I exchange guilty looks. Fortunately, the cops don't spot this because Dad has just asked, "What are you men going to do next?"

"Check the bus schedule, ask some of their drivers, ask a few neighbors. Marty's starting to get worried, you know, but I think we'll fix this up." Meyers shrugs.

"Are you going to put up a search?"

"Eventually, if she doesn't return, yes. Twenty-four hours has to transpire from the time the person goes missing to be able to conduct a search."

"But I'm sure she'll be back by then," Dad says, waving his hand dismissively. "She's probably out shopping at that new mall in Schneider. You know women."

Wilson giggles inappropriately.

"Yeah, that's what we think, too," Meyers says, draining the last of his coffee before getting to his feet.

"So what about the children?" Mom asks, picking up the men's empty coffee mugs.

"The charge of trespassing by Hunter and Lorraine Thomas is pending until we've contacted Esther and heard *her* side of the story," Meyers answers. Then he jokes, grinning, "But we can convict the kids if you want, take 'em off your hands awhile—" Meyers pretends to reach for his handcuffs. Dad guffaws heartily and Mom smiles politely.

The officers move to the door and we follow them. Goodbyes are exchanged; the cops promise to update us tomorrow on any new findings, wink at Lorraine and me, then finally make their exit. I think everyone breathes a sigh of relief as the door closes. I feel weak-kneed and light-headed. Nevertheless, my heart is singing. We pulled it off; the cops have swallowed it!

But as Dad turns to look at us, my smile slides off my face. Dad's trademark scowl is back.

"Now, I don't believe that load of you-know-what you fed to the cops, but they obviously did. Consider yourselves lucky. Now get back to your rooms."

I'm only happy to exit, but Lorraine whines, "Oh, but what about dinner?"

"Your mother will serve it to you in your rooms."

"Is the grounding still on?"

Lorraine looks up at him with a pure face. Dad can't help but relent a little.

"*Shortening* it is under consideration, but only if you two are perfect little angels tonight, got it? Now get back to your rooms."

CHAPTER SIX

DECISIONS, DECISIONS

I scamper away, feeling grateful, with Lorraine following me. We separate in the hallway, and I flop down on my bed, pleasantly exhausted. Today's events have been enough to make anyone weary. In fact, since the school bell had rung signaling the beginning of summer, everything had been pretty crazy. First, terrible Monty's, then the Teleporter, next the break-in, and finally, my first run in with Abottsville's local law enforcement.

Talk about a roller coaster ride! I think to myself, turning over. For the thousandth time today, I wonder where the heck Mrs. H is. I bite my lip, recalling the ominous feeling I got upon first gazing at the Shoe. However, my trepidation had vanished as soon as Lorraine and I had used the Teleporter and found out it actually worked.

But now that I no longer have the Shoe, its magic is beginning to fade. I sit up, musing worriedly. My initial instincts are usually right. What if the Shoe *really* is as dangerous as I had first perceived? What if something bad had happened to Mrs. Hazelton? But before I can reflect on this any longer, my bedroom door bursts open.

I jolt, yelping, but it's only Lorraine. She frowns disapprovingly at me, dressed in her nightgown.

"Oh, honestly, Hunter," she sighs, flouncing over to my bed, "you are so rabbity. How many panic attacks do you have a day—ten, twelve?"

I take my hand off my thudding chest to glare at her. "I've had about five so far, thanks to you. Now get out of my room! You're not allowed in here!"

"Oh, stop being so huffy. I need to talk to you, remember?"

"Yeah, what about?"

"What else? The Teleporter, of course!"

Groaning loudly, I fall back on my bed. "I don't want to talk about that thing."

"Why in the heavens not? You want it back, don't you?"

"I guess..."

"Oh, goodness, you are no fun! *Anyone* would want a Teleporter back; I mean, come on, think of the possibilities—Rome, Greece; I've always wanted to see those old civilizations by the Mediterranean..." She pauses to glare

60

at me. "Oh, just look at my mopey brother. You're such a stick in the mud."

"I am *not* a stick in the mud!"

"Alright then, if you're not, you'll like this new idea I have."

"A new idea?" I sit up warily. Lorraine has that look in her eye...the look I've come to associate with the worst things...

"I think we should go back to that shop again," she declares.

My fears are immediately confirmed.

"What, Monty's?" I croak.

"Yes, that was the name."

"But we can't go back there!" I yelp, struggling to control myself.

"Why in the heavens not?" Lorraine says in the voice of an affronted English woman.

"I don't like the feeling I got from that place. I still can't shake it off."

Lorraine snorts. "A feeling?"

"Alright, an intuition, if you like. If you believe in magic, then you should believe in intuitions."

"*You* should believe in magic too, Hunter. You saw the Teleporter work."

"Okay, okay," I answer wearily. "But how are we going to get to Monty's? We're grounded, remember?"

"Of course I remember," Lorraine snaps. "I wasn't planning on just waltzing through the front door. No—" she continues, her face shining, "we are going to *sneak* out."

I struggle to calm my beating heart as I say faintly, "Sneak out?"

"That's right," she answers loftily. "Of course, if you are going to wimp out, I'll have to go back to the shop alone—"

"But why would you go back to Monty's, anyway?" I cut in. "What good is that going to do?"

"Oh, what else can I do?" Lorraine despairs. "Who knows, maybe there's an extra Teleporter there. I mean, that would make sense, right; a *pair* of shoes? Besides, we can report to that man our shoe was stolen. Possibly we could get a refund."

"But why tonight?" I insist. "The stupid shop won't even be open this late. We'd have to break in."

"Who cares?"

"I care! Number one: it's illegal. Number two: he probably has a security system. Then we'd get caught. We already have a bad record, remember?"

"Number three: Hunter is a big scaredy-cat. Oh, come on, Hunter, do you really think that little shop has a security system? It was practically medieval! Did you see that antique cash register?"

"Whatever," I say. "It's still dangerous. It would be better if we did it in the morning."

"Not with all those silly cops bustling around. They're supposed to start the search for Mrs. Hazelton tomorrow."

"That's at 10:00. We could leave at 8:00, before the cops show up."

"But then Mom and Dad would be up. We'd have to sneak past them in broad daylight."

"Then we wait until they leave for work at 9:00. Don't you understand? The cops can't stop us from going to Monty's. They don't have an area restriction on us."

Lorraine's face falls. All her excuses are gone. "Oh, but," she whimpers, "I just wanted to sneak out tonight because...it would be a bit daring. You know, like an adventure in a book. I've waited my whole life for something exciting like this to happen, and it finally has. I'm not like you. I don't want to be a toad and sit around, trying to do the 'safe' thing. No!" She stands up from my bed in determination, putting a fist over her heart. "I'm willing to risk a little to live! For who can say he has truly lived, until he has known peril!"

"Quiet!" I hiss at Lorraine, whose voice is steadily increasing in volume. "Mom and Dad will hear!"

She turns towards me like a dramatic actress, crying vehemently, "Are you with me, Hunter?!"

"Yes, yes," I say through clenched teeth, shoving her toward the closet as I hear footsteps in the hallway. "Mom and Dad are coming; *hide*!"

As Lorraine comes to her senses and ducks inside, I shut the door behind her. Just then, there's a knock at the door.

"Hunter, I've brought dinner," Mom calls.

"Thanks," I wheeze, making my way back to my bed and collapsing down on it. Mom comes in, carrying a dinner tray.

"I left Lorraine's potpie in her room," she says vaguely as she sets the tray down on my desk. "She's not there, though...remember to bring your dirty dishes back to the sink."

As soon as Mom makes her exit, Lorraine leaves too, giving me a silent look.

I've always enjoyed Mom's chicken potpie, but tonight I am unable to. After taking the dishes back to the sink, I take a long shower, standing there tiredly, letting the spray hit my face. That is, I do until Lorraine starts pounding on the door and complaining that she needs to take a shower, too.

Later that night, I toss and turn under my quilt. Despite my trepidation, I know I can't chicken out now. Lorraine's taunts always get to me. I hate being the baby. But is being a wimp *that* bad? I bite my lip thoughtfully.

Lorraine is always dragging me into dangerous situations because I want to prove to her I'm up to the challenge. But I'm *never* up to the challenge! If I had stuck to my guns and not crossed the street into Monty's I would have been a lot better off because of it. We wouldn't have even bought that cursed Shoe in the first place! *So that's it*, I think, plumping up my pillow, *I'm not going to creep out with Lorraine tonight and go traipsing all over the neighborhood. We will just get in a load of hooey if we do.*

Just then, my door bangs open. I sit up, but don't yell this time. I know it's just stupid Lorraine. But...it's...not!! A giant bulky figure is silhouetted against the doorway. Wildly, I think of A.T. Briner and bolt out of bed, preparing to make a run for it. I'm almost to the window when an oddly familiar, British voice issues from the bulky figure—"Oh, Hunter, you idiot, it's me!"

I freeze, turning back to the doorway.

"Lorraine?"

"Who else would it be, the bogeyman?" Lorraine giggles at her own immature joke as she shuffles to my lamp. As the room is filled with a dim light, I discover the reason for Lorraine's newly acquired bulk. As well as being fully dressed, she is wearing her heaviest winter parker, all buttoned up, with the hood on. What little bit of her face I can see is red, probably from the heat. I roll my eyes.

"What are you wearing *that* for?"

"A disguise," she answers simply. "If anyone sees us tonight, they won't be able to recognize us."

"That's good," I say sarcastically. "I don't want my friends coming up to me tomorrow and asking 'Hunter, I saw you running around in a winter parka last night; what was that all about?'"

"Oh, shut up," Lorraine snips, adjusting her fur-lined cuffs. "You don't want to be caught tonight, do you? Now put on your coat."

I fold my arms. The moment has come. I open my mouth to announce I won't be participating in tonight's illegal events...but nothing comes out.

Lorraine is staring at me expectantly. I have a feeling she won't criticize me this time for wimping out, but I just can't do it. I just can't disappoint her when she's looking so happy. Besides, I don't want her breaking into seedy-looking shops by herself. I have good instincts; I can warn her before something dangerous happens. And if she gets hurt, she'll need an able-bodied person around to call the ambulance. There's no other choice. I will have to go.

I drop my arms to my sides and sigh, "Well, I don't want to go in my parka." I point out the window. "It's sweltering out there! It's summer, in case you've forgotten."

"I haven't forgotten. But I'd rather be a bit stuffy for a few hours than locked in a prison for five years."

I personally feel she's trying to over-dramatize the situation as usual. It's pitch-black and moonless outside. No one is going to recognize us, regardless of whether we are wearing heavy coats or not. Besides, who's going to be outside to see us, anyway? But I decide to agree.

"Okay," I grump, "but get out of my room so I can get dressed first."

As soon as she shuffles out, I pull off my pajamas and dress nervously in jeans and a shirt. As I'm tying my shoelaces, I glance up at my clock. 11:36 p.m. Already draped in dread, I put on my winter parka, buttoning it up and flipping the hood on. Lorraine comes back in, looking excited.

"Let's go," she whispers, moving to the window and sliding it open. She goes out first, landing below on the ground on the side of our house. It's my turn next. Like a man walking the plank, I drag myself over to the window and boost myself over the ledge. I'm having a little   trouble getting over— my cursed parka is constraining most movement. But I manage to land with a thud beside Lorraine. She nods at me. Operation Invade Monty's has begun.

CHAPTER SEVEN

OPERATION INVADE MONTY'S

Lorraine automatically takes the lead as we move through the backyard. We clamber over our fence and drop into the alleyway below. My parka is already ripped, I'm sweating like a hog, and my heart is beating a drum roll against my ribs. But I try to ignore all this as we continue our progress down the alleyway.

As we pass someone's backyard, a dog barks shrilly behind the fence. I nearly shed my skin, but Lorraine shoves me, muttering, "Oh, honestly, Hunter, I wouldn't have brought you along if I knew you were going to jump at every little noise like this."

"You know how I am!" I hiss back at her. All the neighborhood dogs have joined in the barking now; I'm praying no one comes out to investigate. However, we manage to make it out of the alleyway and onto Worchester Drive.

"Just a few more blocks," Lorraine says in a hushed voice, brushing perspiration off her face in a lady-like manner.

Abottsville is a quiet town, so there's no one out. Even so, the now familiar sense of prophetic doom is filling me. *You are definitely going to regret this later,* I tell myself as Lorraine and I are forced to duck behind a mailbox as a car passes. As the vehicle's taillights disappear around a corner, we both straighten up, relieved.

"Let's go," Lorraine says, and we start to sneak along again, keeping close to the buildings. Before I know it, the ramshackle shop of Monty's is leaning leeringly towards us in the dark. My heart starts hammering so loudly against my chest that I'm surprised Lorraine's not telling me off about it.

"I can't believe I'm doing this," I mumble at her.

"Shh!" she remonstrates, looking very serious for once. We move around to the back of the street, where the absence of street lights has made it deathly dark. The store's simple wooden wall doesn't seem to have an escape hatch or exit, just a door squashed in the left corner.

"Did you bring a flashlight?" I whisper.

She nods and pats a lump in her pocket. Then she whispers back, "Here's the plan—we both get in and begin looking around for the second Shoe. Once we find it—" She

69

pauses to take some things out of her pocket. The first thing is twenty-three dollars, stapled to a hand-written letter. Next, there's a second letter.

"Once we find it," she repeats, "we'll put the money and the letter on his desk next to the cash register, then leave."

"Okay. What does the letter say?"

"Oh, it's just explaining our situation with Mrs. Hazelton. I'm sure he'll understand."

I don't share Lorraine's confidence, but it's too late now.

"What's the other letter for?" I ask, pointing to it.

"That's for if we can't find the Shoe tonight. In this letter, I am simply asking him to reimburse us with the twenty-three dollars I previously paid. I'm also asking him to restock a few more Teleporters if he's run out."

This is probably the most ridiculous situation I've ever been in. I might have laughed if I wasn't so frightened.

"How are we going to get in?" I ask, brushing some sweat out of my eyes.

Lorraine starts stuffing everything back in her pocket and points to the rickety door.

"There."

We move toward it, Lorraine in front. Heat presses down on my heavily insulated self as I stupidly watch her yank at the door handle.

"Oh, it's locked," she puffs disappointedly.

"You should have expected that," I point out.

When she glares at me, I say, "What? He's not going to leave it open so people like us can walk in, is he?"

"What do you mean, 'people like us'?"

"Burglars. 'cause that's what we are now, you know."

She humphs and turns back to the door, apparently thinking hard. At that very moment, I suddenly get that feeling you *never* want to get if: a) you're a highly nervous person, b) planning a break-in, c) in the dead of the night. Something unseen is watching us...

My heart freezes and my breath stops as the skin on the back of my neck prickles. I don't dare turn around as I struggle to regain use of my vocal cords.

"*Lorraine!*" I manage to croak out.

"What is it, Hunter?" she snaps back, totally oblivious to my terror. Then it happens. Only an inch away from my ear, someone behind me says softly...

"And what might you two young people be doing?"

These sinisterly spoken words bring my seized body back into action. Leaping into the air, I let out a scream that echoes through the alley and barrel straight into a horrified Lorraine.

We both collide against the closed door and fall in a heap on the ground. Struggling to get to my feet, I discover that I am unable to. Due to all the extra padding, my arms seem to be locked in the outward position. Curse these constraining parkas! Beside me, Lorraine appears to be struggling with the same problem. As a result, we are both forced to lie like a couple of fishes, staring up in panic at the terrible form of A.T. Briner.

"Well, well, well," he sneers as his eyes gleam visibly in the dark. Stroking his goatee, he continues, "What have we here? Two delinquent children attempting to break into my shop in the dead of the night? That can't be good—not good for them, I mean." He snickers sinisterly.

"Please don't hurt us!" I squeak.

"We didn't mean to!" Lorraine cries, and I notice somewhat vaguely that her accent has disappeared. "Don't you remember us?"

"Remember you?" The man stops stroking his goatee to stare at us.

"Yes," she answers hurriedly, managing to get to her feet and pulling me up with her. My trembling knees buckle a little and I hang desperately onto her shoulder; I'm making an effort not to faint.

"We were browsing in your shop two days ago," she goes on. "We bought a shoe, remember?"

The man continues to stare at her. "Oh, *now* I recall it! But—" he frowns, "I thought that you were British."

Lorraine clears her throat, quickly returning to the old aristocratic accent. "Oh, but I am. And you remember my brother, Hunter?" She gestures to me, still hanging green-faced onto her parka.

"Yes, of course," the man answers smoothly, smiling. He is obviously feeling more charitable to us now that he's realized we were once paying customers. He probably doesn't get a lot of buyers.

"Would you like to come in?" he asks, gesturing to the shop.

"If you would be so kind," Lorraine encourages him politely.

He moves easily past us toward the door, producing a key. Lorraine makes to follow him, but I stay where I am. I have reason to be wary of A.T. Briner. Questions spin around in my head. Why do his eyes gleam so strangely in the dark? How did he appear so suddenly behind us? Where did he come from? And why is he out fully-dressed in the middle of the night?

Perhaps the always-ignorant-Lorraine hadn't noticed these suspicious signs, but I certainly had. And unless I want both of us killed, I am going to have to take matters into my own hands.

"No," I announce, surprising even myself.

"No what?" Lorraine asks curiously.

I turn and force myself to look into the man's eerie eyes.

"No, Lorraine and I will have to decline the invitation into your shop," I tell him calmly, pushing up my parka sleeve to glance at my watch. It reads 12:15 a.m. "You are very courteous but I'm afraid that both of us are wanted at home. It's after twelve now, you know."

"How very inconvenient for you," Briner says, inclining his head. "And I cannot keep you from your summons."

"No," Lorraine snaps. Now she's looking at me. I can't discern her features in the dark, but I bet she's angry. "We aren't wanted at home, Mr.—ahh..."

"Briner."

"Yes, we *are*," I insist. I consider dragging Lorraine away by force, but quickly reject the idea. I hardly have enough strength to stand up on my own, due to fear and heat-exhaustion. Why in the heck had I decided to come on this little jaunt? I'm never good in life-threatening situations like this! I struggle to pull myself together. My heart is beating like a caged monkey, my head is throbbing, and perspiration is blurring my already limited night-vision.

"Can I *please* talk to you alone?" I grind out at Lorraine through clenched teeth.

"Fine," she snaps, sounding harassed. "Mr. Briner, would you mind?"

"Not in the least."

Lorraine and I move into a corner out of earshot of the man.

"Are you insane?" I whisper fiercely at her.

"I must be," she shoots back. "I don't even know why I let you come along with me! I should have known you would be like this, paranoid as usual—"

"I'm not paranoid."

"You're not dry, you're not a wimp, you're not paranoid. Then what are you, Hunter?"

"I'm intelligent, for one. And if I'm not intelligent, then at least I have a little common sense."

"Oh, you *are* being dry now."

I jerk my head over to the man, who is still watching us through the darkness. "Do you really trust him? What if he lets us into the shop, then locks us in and kills us?"

"Oh, now you're being melodramatic. And disgusting." She makes a face. "Anyway, there's only one of him, and two of us."

"Yeah, but he's an adult. And he's not a normal adult!"

"Hunter, listen." She's speaking slowly and clearly now, as if I'm an idiot. "The reason we took this trip over here was to get the Teleporter back. Now, if you don't actually want to go into the shop, that's fine."

"But I don't want you to go in, either!" I blurt.

"Fine. I won't go in, either. I'll simply ask the man to go inside the store and retrieve the Teleporter himself. If there isn't one available, hopefully he'll reimburse us."

"I don't think he's going to be nice enough to reimburse us."

"Fine. But I might as well ask him since there's a bit of a chance, right? Now come over here and let's cut a deal with him."

Feeling slightly relieved, but still tense, I follow Lorraine's bulk back to where Briner is standing by the door.

"Oh, you're probably wondering what Hunter and I are doing here tonight," she begins pleasantly to him.

"Well, it would be rather nice to know."

"It starts out with the Teleporter you sold us two days ago." She pauses. "Unfortunately, before we had time to use the object, it was stolen from us."

"Was it?"

"Oh, yes," she answers as I nod by her side. "It was stolen by our next door neighbor, a woman named Mrs. Hazelton. She promptly used the devise, transporting herself to a place or places unknown."

"That would be Florida, of course," the man says.

Lorraine blinks. "Florida?"

"That's correct; it was earlier today. I assumed it was you and your young brother whom had teleported to Florida. Now I realize that this was impossible, for you yourselves have not yet employed the object."

"Mrs. Hazelton is in Florida?!" I squawk.

"As I have said, that's correct."

"But how do you know?" Lorraine blurts.

76

"I know absurdly easily. The shoe is marked with a tracking device. Would you like to see how I track the Teleporter's progress?"

"Ooh, of course!" Lorraine squeals, clapping her hands together like she's about to receive a gigantic surprise.

"The map is inside my office," Briner explains, pointing to the door. My heart, whose pulse-rate had managed to descend to the level of a hyperactive dog's, now soars to new heights.

"Now wait just a minute!" I shout, forcing myself once again to look into the man's eerie eyes. "Just why are you so anxious to hustle us into your shop?"

"Perhaps you misread my motives, young man," he replies, inclining his head. "Although you perceive them to be cruel, I assure you they are not. You are free to enter at my invitation and good intention; I will not force you, certainly."

There is a long pause. Lorraine and I glance at each other, then back to Briner. He has extended his hand toward the door and seems to be waiting.

Lorraine raises her chin to a proper height. "Mr. Briner," she declares in her best British accent, "we would be happy to come inside."

I swallow, but make no complaint. It's too late now; Briner has already slid the key into the lock, and the rickety door of the shop creaks open.

CHAPTER EIGHT

SOME BUSINESS DEALINGS

A pitch-black interior greets us, the slightly sweet smell of aged dust rising up to meet our nostrils. I jump a little as the door closes. The man makes a movement in his corner and a lamp is switched on, filling the shop with a dim yellow light. Knees shaking slightly, I look around.

It looks the same as it did two days ago, only maybe a little bit more forbidding. There are the tilting bookshelves in the middle of the room, crammed with dusty volumes; somber portraits hanging on the walls, old globes and maps everywhere, strange objects lining one wall, and near the other wall, the man's cluttered desk, paperweights clumped everywhere. Briner is leaning against that very desk now, watching us as we stand in the doorway.

"I hope I'm not being too rude to ask," he says, "but I can't help but wonder why the two of you are wearing winter parkas."

We both blush; I realize I'm sweating like a polar bear in South Africa. As we tear out of our padding, I feel an enormous relief as the weight is literally lifted off my shoulders. Lorraine is explaining stupidly, "Oh...you know...nights can be a bit drafty...in June."

"Well, I suppose that is possible," Briner concedes, pushing away from his desk. At this moment, Lorraine suddenly seems to remember why we risked this little stroll into Monty's.

"Oh!" she exclaims. "What about the—"

"The map?" the man finishes, smiling in a way that shows his pointed teeth. "Are you ready to see it?"

"Yes, of course," Lorraine bubbles eagerly.

He motions to her and moves around his desk. Lorraine hurries over, pulling me with her. Behind the man's desk is a door I hadn't noticed last time. It's small, with red paint peeling off it. For some reason, the sight of it causes a doomful feeling to rise in my chest.

Lorraine has dragged me into another hooey-load of trouble, I think to myself darkly. *Did Hunter Thomas have any backbone?* I definitely should have put my foot down about not coming here. But here I am, thanks to my lack of that necessary spinal structure.

"Just a moment," Briner snips smoothly, ducking inside the door and shutting it behind him. Immediately, I turn to Lorraine.

"Look at this horrible situation you've forced us into!" I hiss furiously.

"Oh, stuff it!" she hisses back. "We are this close—" (she holds up a thumb and forefinger) "—to getting the Teleporter back! So stop acting like a blathering idiot!"

"Okay, so first I'm dry, and now I'm a blathering idiot. I wish you'd make up your mind."

"Well, now you sound dry."

Just then, the door swings back open and we fall silent. A.T. Briner has reappeared, holding a rolled-up piece of parchment in his hand.

"Now *this*," he says, pushing some papers out of the way to spread the parchment on his desk, "is something I have dubbed the Teleportation Tracker. Or the T.T., if you like."

Lorraine giggles immaturely at the abbreviation. I glare at her. This is not a time for infantile humor. Briner seems to be thinking the same thing as he clears his throat in disapproval.

I look back at the map. Although it appears old, it seems to be depicting the modern world, as far as I can see. However, I do notice something weird in the right-hand corner. There's a small box in the wide margin, depicting some sort of landform I don't recognize.

"What's that?" I ask, pointing to it.

Briner clears his throat again, but not in the same manner. "*That*," he repeats, "is an island."

"An island? Why isn't it in the ocean with the others?" I ask, starting to get a little suspicious. Is it just me, or is the man avoiding my gaze?

"Because it was just recently discovered."

"Recently discovered? How recently? We've known all the islands on earth for a while now."

Briner frowns. "Don't be so presumptuous, young man. There is still much to be known of this planet, the many mysteries of its form yet to be unfolded."

There is a pause as we both stare at each other. What is this man talking about? I grimace; he sounds like some corny—

Lorraine, as if unable to stand the suspense, breaks into my thoughts.

"Ooh, an uncharted island," she says, rubbing her hands together excitedly. "Is that where Mrs. Hazelton is now?"

"No," Briner answers, his tone becoming brisk and efficient again. "She is here." He points to Florida of the United States, and I notice a miniscule red dot glowing around Tampa Bay.

"Oh, I see!" Lorraine says with sudden insight. "The dot signifies Mrs. Hazelton. In *Florida*!"

81

"Duh," I grump. I'm still feeling quite peeved. I glance back at the right-hand corner of the map, but the island doesn't seem to have any markings or words around it. With a sigh, I turn back to Florida, thinking to myself, *another unsolved mystery to add to the rest.*

"Yes, that is exactly right," Briner says, ignoring my 'duh' comment.

"Oh," Lorraine sighs, "I do wish I could get that Shoe back. Mind you, I did pay for it, and I haven't even used it yet."

"That's extremely unfortunate for you," Briner says, though he isn't looking particularly sympathetic. In fact, his eyes are glittering strangely.

"Do you really want the Shoe back?" he asks in a quiet voice.

"Oh, of course!" Lorraine says, clasping her hands. "Or another one just like it. Perhaps you have a few more for sale."

"I'm terribly sorry," the man says, smiling in a way I don't like. "I have none for sale or in stock. I'm afraid you bought my only Teleporter from me yesterday." He glances at his watch. "Well, technically *two* days ago."

"Oh, I'm so disappointed," Lorraine sniffs. "Perhaps...you would be so kind...as to reimburse Hunter and I our twenty-three dollars."

"If I remember correctly," Briner says sneeringly, "you only paid twenty-two dollars and eighty-five cents. You were a bit short. But of course, I am willing to reimburse you for a stolen good—if indeed that is all you wish to settle for..."

"What do you mean?" Lorraine asks quickly.

"What I mean is, are you satisfied with the return of a meager twenty-two dollars and eighty-five cents—or would you rather have the Shoe itself?"

"The Shoe itself, of course!" Lorraine squeals.

The man leans forward across the desk, staring at us with his strange greenish eyes. "Then I shall have it returned to you."

"How's that?" I ask, my heart thumping loudly in my chest as a disturbing (yet quite possible) scenario runs through my head. Briner, catching the first flight to Florida, scouring the whole of Tampa Bay to find Mrs. Hazelton. Finding her one dark night in the hallway of Holiday Inn as she fumbles with her hotel key to put it in the lock, the dirty brown shoe peeking out of her handbag. Briner creeping stealthily toward her, one hand raised, a knife gleaming in his fist....

I make a loud choking noise. "You're not going to-"

"To what?" the man asks, straightening up.

"Oh, you're going to go after her, aren't you?" Lorraine gasps. "Hunter and I want to go, too! Florida, I've never been, how adventurous—"

"Shut up, Lorraine," I snap, rolling my eyes. *God, does she have any sense?!*

"Now, now, Mr. Thomas," the man says reprovingly. "There's no need for that kind of outburst."

Lorraine sniffs loudly at me, but I sneer at her.

"Lorraine, *hello*...we're not going to Florida."

"Really? Who says?"

"I say! As your brother, I have a right—"

Lorraine shoves me away. "Oh, shut up, Hunter! Mr. Briner and I are making plans. So if you don't wish to come along with us to Florida and have a little fun for once, then you can stay here in Abottsville and rot the whole summer away! See if I care!"

I open my mouth to fire back a terrible retort, but A.T. Briner breaks in, clearing his throat.

"Ah, excuse me, children; I hate to break up such as rousing argument, but I'm afraid *neither* of you are going to Florida."

There is a long silence as Lorraine stares at the man and I stare at her, feeling a strange relief.

"Wh-what do you mean?" she stammers finally, her face falling. "I thought—"

"I'm terribly sorry," Briner apologizes, clasping his hands in front of him, "but such a trip would be impossible. What would your parents think if you were to just suddenly pack your bags and head for the east coast?"

"Oh," Lorraine says in a small voice, coming back to reality for the first time all night, "I suppose they would be a bit bewildered."

"Yeah, a bit," I smirk.

Lorraine turns back to glare at me, but Briner, as if trying to head off another argument, says quickly, "Of course, I am sure there will be other, more convenient times for you and your brother to enjoy a vacation."

"I doubt it," Lorraine answers sadly. "Our family isn't very big on trips."

"Excuse me," I say loudly, "but aren't we getting off the central topic? What about the Shoe?"

"Ah yes, the Shoe." Briner runs one hand over the map on his desk. "*One* of this party will be traveling to Florida to retrieve the item."

"Will you send us a postcard, at least?" Lorraine asks hopefully.

Briner smiles. "Why yes, of course I can."

"How exactly are you planning to get to Florida?" I ask him, still a little suspicious.

"By finding a means of transportation, naturally," the man answers. "A broomstick, perhaps, or—"

"Wait, a broomstick!" I yelp. "How does *that* work?"

"Well, I'm sure you have seen its operation on the movies and television—"

"Yes, on *movies* and *television*. That's exactly right!" I press my hands against my temples. "On a screen, where it's all imaginary! Are you telling me you actually *have* a broomstick?"

Lorraine sighs in exasperation at my side. "Oh, why is that so hard to believe, Hunter?" she asks. "I mean, you've seen Mr. Briner's Teleporter work. Why can't he have a broomstick, too?"

I shake my head, trying to throw off the feeling that I'm slowly going insane.

"Alright," I finally answer with some weariness, looking back at Briner. "But if you *are* planning to go from here to Florida, how are you going to do it without anyone seeing you?"

"Oh, I know!" Lorraine answers eagerly for him. "You have an invisibility cloak, don't you?"

"Not a cloak, exactly," the man answers. "I find them too cumbersome. And especially heavy during summer! No, I have this—"

I back up as Mr. Briner walks past us from around his desk, heading to the corner of the shop. Lorraine follows, pulling me along. We both watch him as he bends down over an old chest on the floor, pushing open the lid. There's an old linen cloth lying at the bottom of the chest, and I frown. Is this guy going to wear a *sheet*? But Briner pushes back the sheet and picks up a small vial lying within its folds. As he holds the vial up to the light, I see that it is full of a pale greenish liquid. The man uncorks it, glancing towards us.

I gulp suddenly; it looks like poison. But surely he wouldn't—

"Oh, what is it?" Lorraine asks, leaning forward. I pull her back as Briner straightens up.

"This—" he gives the vial a sniff, "is an invisibility concoction, recently invented by my own brother, Eugene. It works quite well, actually. Three drops on the tongue for an hour of obscurity."

"Oh," she says in an almost longing voice, "how does it taste? Can I try some?"

I open my mouth to protest, but to my relief, the man shakes his head.

"I'm sorry, Miss Thomas, but I'm afraid I must save the vial's contents for my journey to Florida. Which should be starting in..." he glances at his watch, "one hour."

"Oh, one hour," Lorraine groans. "Why can't you leave now?"

The man studies us. I can't help but notice that the sinister light is creeping back into his eyes.

"Because," he answers slowly, "I have a bit of unfinished business left to take care of here."

"Unfinished business with whom?" Lorraine asks curiously.

Briner bends his head, sliding the small vial into an inside suit pocket.

"Well," he answers, "business with *you*, actually."

87

CHAPTER NINE

A BROWN PAPER BAG

My mouth goes dry. Beside me, I hear Lorraine say, "Do you mean business with *me*, or business with Hunter *and* I?"

I moan, grabbing her arm. "Lorraine, you idiot, don't you understand what he means?"

Lorraine glares at me, pulling herself out of my grip. "No, I don't understand! Mr. Briner hasn't even said what he wants from us yet!"

"Well, I know what he wants from us!" I turn around to glare at Briner. He stares back at me, his hands clasped in front of him.

"*Well*, Mr. Thomas," he asks after a terrible pause, "what do I want?"

I open my mouth, but can't seem to be able to answer him. He sighs, almost wearily, then turns away from me.

"I tire of your suspicions, Mr. Thomas, which have been evident since we first met two days ago. What do you expect of me? Something terrible, quite obviously."

He begins to move, pacing around Lorraine and me. I drag her closer, keeping him in my sight as he circles. Lorraine has fallen silent; she's staring at him, too.

"Alas, it's human nature, for one to question and fear what he considers *unusual. Strange.*"

"D-d-dangerous?" I stammer.

The man stops, facing us. "Only dangerous if you make it to be. And you have made it to be, Mr. Thomas. I'm afraid you leave me with no choice."

"But I haven't done anything!" I cry, stumbling backward. To my surprise, Lorraine steps in front of me, blocking me from Briner.

He stops, his eyebrows raised. "Not you as well, Lorraine? I thought that you trusted me."

"I do trust you, Mr. Briner." She glances back at me and I notice that her accent has disappeared. "But what are you going to do with Hunter?"

"Nothing *painful*," he answers, "as your younger brother seems so badly to fear. Only this."

He pulls a small brown paper bag out of his pocket, its top folded over.

I choke. "What is that?! What's in there?!"

Briner sneers. "Didn't I tell you this wouldn't be painful?"

He takes a step closer and I drop to my knees behind Lorraine.

"Get up, Hunter," she snaps, prodding me hard with her foot. "He said it wouldn't hurt!"

"And you believe this guy?!"

From around her waist, I see Briner roll his eyes. "This is exactly the type of behavior I was speaking about," he says, unfolding the bag. "Now come out here and take a handful of this Amnesia Dust!"

"Am-amnesia Dust?"

"Yes!"

"But what if I don't want—"

"Oh, wait," Lorraine breaks in, her accent returning. "What does Hunter need Amnesia Dust for?"

The man sighs. "Perhaps I should start at the beginning," he says. "As you do or don't know, my shop opened about a week ago. My first customer was an eager young man, who happened to purchase my Genie of the Lamp—"

"Oh my," Lorraine breaks in. "You have a *genie*?!"

"Don't interrupt him," I growl through clenched teeth.

"Fine then." She gives me a quick glare. "Please continue, Mr. Briner."

Briner clears his throat. "Well, as I was saying, the customer happened to purchase the lamp. However, he returned to the shop a few days later with some complaints. Apparently, the genie had been defective. The man was quite upset about this and he threatened me. He made some hints about deceptive trade practices, and possibly a lawsuit. Of course, this could not be allowed."

Briner pauses, looking at both of us. "Business in Magic is a delicate operation," he continues, "and it can not afford to be disrupted. You see, my shop is handled quite carefully. I have placed many wards around it, which prevents those unworthy from entering it. Unfortunately, the wards are not fool-proof, as Mr. Thomas and my previous customer have shown. And look what it caused! Nearly a lawsuit! As I said before, such a thing could not be allowed. I was forced to...ah...dispose of the man."

I gasp. "Dispose?!"

"Don't worry," Briner answers quickly. "You will not be subject to such an, ah...cumbersome method. No, my brother Eugene has recently devised something much more effective." He holds up the paper bag. "Amnesia Dust! The victim simply takes a whiff and the memory of Monty's and Monty's products is quickly erased."

"No way!" I cry, straightening up. "I'm not taking that stuff. That's messing with people's minds! Their memories! It's dangerous!"

91

The man's face darkens. "I'm afraid you have no choice, Mr. Thomas."

"Oh, yeah?" Half-terrified, half-raging, I step out from behind Lorraine. My heart is pounding hard through my t-shirt. "What are you gonna do? Keep me in this shop until I take it? I don't think so."

"Hunter—" I hear Lorraine say from behind me, but I ignore her. Glaring into the man's greenish eyes, I watch him as he takes a step toward me.

"I can't let you leave in this state, Mr. Thomas. You're a danger. A danger to yourself, to me, and to your sister, Lorraine. Take the Dust."

"No."

"Yes."

"No!"

"Don't make me force you—"

"ARRGGHH!"

Screaming in fear and rage, I grab Lorraine, dart around the man, and go sprinting for the door. I've almost made it—but Briner is quicker than I bargained for. With a wild leap, he springs in front of us. Grabbing my shirt collar, he drags me away from Lorraine.

"Help!" I choke at her. Briner is shoving the open paper bag in my face, snarling, "Take it!"

I clamp my fingers over my nose, refusing to take a breath of the gold dust that's floating out. At that moment, a fast-moving streak crosses my vision. It's Lorraine! She rams hard into my captor's side, knocking him backward. I'm ripped from his grip and fall to my knees. Jerking my head up, I watch in horror and amazement as the paper bag goes sailing into the air and makes a sharp descent—towards Briner.

It lands right on his head, spewing glittering gold dust all over his face. He gasps, chokes, and sneezes, staggering backward. Jumping to my feet, I watch as the man takes his last breath, then collapses abruptly to the floor.

There's a long moment of silence as the dust settles. Then I glance towards Lorraine, and notice that we're both holding our noses.

"Whew!" She drops her hand. "That was a close one!"

"Yeah," I say, "and now it's time to go."

I wobble across the floor towards her and grab her arm. For some reason, my knees are shaking and my voice is coming out high and squeaky.

"Come on, Lorraine, let's go."

I start towards the door, but she pulls me back.

"Wait, Hunter."

"For what?"

"For Mr. Briner! What if he's hurt?"

"But we *want* him to be hurt!" I plead, tugging on her arm. "Let's get out of this place!"

"No, Hunter!" She jerks out of my grip, and to my horror, starts walking back to the man.

"Get back here!" I cry, clutching my chest. "Don't go near him! Who cares? Did you just see what that guy did to me? He tried to *kill* me!"

Lorraine turns back to me, her face pale and strange-looking. "He tried to kill you?"

"Well, you saw the dust, didn't you? How are we supposed to know it was just Amnesia Dust? Maybe it was something deadly! Lorraine, what are you doing?" (She's dropped to her knees beside Briner.) "Hello, I said *deadly*!"

"I know," she answers, looking back at me again. "And he got covered in the stuff. Maybe it killed him. We have to make sure he's alright."

"But Lorraine—"

"Do you want him to be dead, Hunter? Because I don't! I don't want to be responsible for this!"

I stare at Lorraine. I can't think of anything else to say. It's obvious she's really worried. Despite the fact that I want to sprint right out of the shop and never look back, I force myself to stay. Stay and watch her bend over the man's prone form, checking for a pulse. Then she straightens up and looks back at me.

"Well?" I ask her, feeling tense in spite of myself. *What if he really is dead?*

"His heart is still beating."

"Uh, he's still breathing—I guess?"

94

Lorraine brushes some glittery dust off his nose and mouth, then gets back to her feet.

"Yes, but very faintly."

"That's good, right? That means we can go now, right?" I grab the door handle.

"Not yet," she answers grimly.

"But *why* not? Please?"

She glares at me. "We're not just going to leave him here. What if—"

Suddenly, there's a groaning sound. I scream, jumping back against the door.

"L-Lorraine, he's getting up!"

Sure enough, the man is stirring on the floor, his arms and legs moving weakly. He groans again.

"Lorraine, let's get the heck out of here while we still have the chance. Come on—" I swing open the door, "we're this close!"

"Shut up, Hunter." She takes a step toward Briner. "Oh, Mr. Briner, are you okay?"

The man's eyes flicker open. I watch in frozen horror as he pushes himself into a sitting position.

"Oh," he moans, holding his head, "where am I?"

CHAPTER TEN

BRINER'S BETTER BEHAVIOR

Lorraine and I exchange quick glances.

"Well, Mr. Briner," Lorraine answers him, now sounding like a patient English nanny, "you happen to be in—"

"Wait a moment," Briner breaks in, staring at us, "who are you two?"

"Well, we're—"

"You're not *my* children, are you?"

"Well, no." Lorraine blushes. "I am Lorraine Thomas and this is my brother, Hunter."

"Oh!" Briner says, then looks somewhat embarrassed. "Not that it would be terribly *bad* if you were my children. You look like quite nice children. It's just that I don't think I'm quite ready—" Suddenly, he stops talking, then glances around. "This is not *your* home is it?"

"Well...uh..."

"If it is, then I am sorry for intruding. I'm not sure how I came to be here, actually—and what is this dust doing all over me?!"

He begins to brush it off his face and shoulders quickly. Lorraine and I stare at him. *So it* was *Amnesia Dust*, I think to myself. Of course, that poses a new problem.

A.T. makes an unsteady effort to stand. Lorraine moves forward to help him, and I feel my jaw clench. She seems to be forgetting how viciously the man attacked me only five minutes ago. Not that he is looking particularly dangerous now, but still: who knows what is going to happen next? And there's also the fact that I hold grudges.

With my sister's (unnecessary) aid, Briner goes around to his desk to sit down on his high-backed chair.

I force myself to edge forward, noticing up close how the man's eyes seem to be unfocused. He smiles vaguely at Lorraine. His new behavior is obviously a side-effect of the Dust. I wonder when it will wear off.

"So," Lorraine walks back around the desk to stand beside me, "what exactly *can* you remember, Mr. Briner?"

"Well," he mutters in a vague voice, rubbing his goatee. "I do remember that my name is Artmas Tybalt Briner. And I was born on July 23rd, 1968. And I have a younger brother named Edward. Or is it Eugene?...Oh, yes, it is Eugene!" He looks back at us, smiling.

"Okay, how many fingers am I holding up?" Lorraine asks, raising her hand.

"Oh, for God's sake," I mutter.

"Four!" Briner answers, looking proud of himself.

"Lorraine, can I talk to you a minute, *alone*?" I growl at her.

She sighs in exasperation. "Hunter, can't you see I am trying to make an analysis of this man's condition?"

"Yes, but I need to talk to you now. Mr. Briner, do you mind?"

"No, not at all." He smiles vaguely over my left shoulder.

"Come on, Lorraine." I lead her away, over to the bookcases.

"What is it, Hunter?"

"It's just that you seem to be forgetting one little thing over there. That man attacked me! If I hadn't gotten away, then it would be *me* sitting in that chair instead of him!"

She smirks, sticking her face in mine. "Oh, and how exactly did you 'get away,' smart man?"

"I—"

"I saved you, remember, Hunter? I knocked Mr. Briner out of the way!"

I stare at her. "Oh yeah, yeah, you did."

"Exactly. So let me handle this." She starts to push past me, but I pull her back.

"Wait a second, I'm not done yet."

I glance to where Briner is seated at his desk, staring past the cash register in a daze.

"It was Amnesia Dust, obviously," I say finally. "And Briner got quite a lot of it. An overdose, probably. That explains this funny mood of his. And how he can't remember his brother's name."

"Oh, excellent deductions," Lorraine says sarcastically.

I frown at her. "Yeah? But we don't know this. How long is his amnesia going to last?"

"I'm not sure. How long *does* amnesia last?"

"In this case, probably forever."

"Oh no," she groans. "What if you're right? How will Mr. Briner be able to run his shop if he can't remember anything about it?"

"Well, I'm not too worried about this place, if you want to know the truth," I answer, looking around the creepy room.

Lorraine frowns. "Really, Hunter, you need to stop being so selfish."

"Me, *selfish*?! Lorraine, this shop has been trouble for us since we stepped inside that day! You've got to admit that now! Look at what that man almost did to me!" I point to the torn bag on the floor. "I told you he was dangerous!

But you know what? I'm glad I came here tonight. Because if I hadn't, *you* might have never come out!"

Lorraine stares at me, looking as if she's about to say something else. But just then, the man calls behind us, "Children, children, I have remembered something else!"

Lorraine ducks around the bookcase, hurrying back toward him. I hang back for a moment, then follow her reluctantly.

"Oh, well," she asks him, "what do you remember?"

Briner looks away from her, giving me a dazed look. Then he points at me with his finger.

"That I don't like him."

I groan inwardly. *This can't be good.*

"Oh, Mr. Briner," Lorraine cries, "what's not to like about Hunter?"

He shrugs. "I don't know. I just don't like him." Then he turns to my sister, adding almost reluctantly, "And I remember I don't like you, either."

Lorraine puts her hand over her heart. "Oh, but I have been so nice to you, Mr. Briner!"

"Yeah, but you knocked him over, remember?" I mutter into her ear.

She pushes me away, then says, "But we like *you*, Mr. Briner."

"I know." He puts his hands over his forehead. "It is all so confusing. A blur inside my head...I can't recall anything..." He glances up at us hopefully. "Perhaps you can tell me what happened. What I forgot."

Before Lorraine can open her mouth, I pinch her arm hard, hissing in her ear, "Don't tell him anything!" The less this man knows, the better, in my opinion.

Now Briner sits up straight. "What are you two whispering about? Not about me, are you?" His voice becomes injured. "You shouldn't keep secrets from me."

"Oh, of course we're not, Mr. Briner," Lorraine says consolingly, then turns back to me. "We'll have to tell him sooner or later, Hunter."

"Tell me what?" he asks anxiously.

"Oh, well, sir...Mr. Briner," Lorraine sighs, clasping her hands in front of her. I suppress a groan as she takes a deep breath. She's going to tell. What will the man do when he hears what happened to him in his shop only ten minutes ago?

"Perhaps I should start at the beginning," she says finally. "Mr. Briner, you opened a shop here last week, in Abottsville, New Hampshire. It's called Monty's and it's a magic shop. It sells magical products. Hunter and I came in two days ago and bought a Teleporter from you."

"Wait a moment," he breaks in. "What is a Teleporter?"

"Um, well," Lorraine glances at me, "it's a devise, in the form of an old shoe, only it has the ability to transport you from place to place. It's quite a—"

"Oh, I see, it's magic!" Briner says, then smiles wistfully. "I have always loved magic! In fact, as a boy—" Suddenly he stops talking, then bursts out, "Wait, I have remembered something else!"

"What is it?" Lorraine asks quickly.

"My brother Eugene!" he answers. "He will know how to get me out of this fix!"

"Oh, good," she says. "Do you know how to contact him?"

"Contact him?"

"Yes, does he have a telephone number?"

"Telephone number?"

I groan loudly. "Lorraine, he doesn't know what any of that stuff is."

"Yes, I do," Briner says, frowning. "It is only that Eugene and I have never communicated by telephone. We use a much more effective method than that."

"What is the method?" Lorraine asks.

"The Glass," he answers mysteriously.

"What's that?" I ask, but Briner doesn't answer. He stands up, looking around his desk.

"Is the Glass in the shop?" Lorraine asks.

"I am not sure." Briner picks up a paperweight and looks under it. "Perhaps it is here....or perhaps at my house."

"Where is your house?"

Briner stops, looking suddenly stricken. "I can't remember!"

"Well, do you think it's near here?" she asks, sounding almost as worried as he does.

"I have an idea," I say suddenly. "Maybe Mr. Briner lives *in* the shop. That's why he can't remember."

Lorraine frowns at me. "That's stupid. How can he live in his own shop? Where's his bed? Where's his bathroom?"

"Maybe he doesn't even need that stuff," I answer. "Come on, Lorraine, you have to admit this man is not a normal human being."

Briner glares darkly at us. "I wish you two would stop speaking about me as if I'm not even here."

"I'm sorry, Mr. Briner," Lorraine apologizes. "I'm sure the information will come to you."

Just then, I spot the small door behind the man's desk. "Look!" I say. "I can't believe I forgot about this. Maybe the man lives behind his desk!"

As Briner looks behind him, Lorraine says, "Maybe you should try it, Mr. Briner."

"I suppose I haven't any other choice," Briner answers, then pushes open the red door. I crane my neck around, trying to see what lies beyond it. There's only a long stone corridor, twisting and turning out of sight.

Briner steps over the threshold and the torches along the walls suddenly spring to life, making me jump backward. Lorraine rolls her eyes. The man looks back at us, his form silhouetted by the wavering reddish light.

"Are you coming along as well?" he asks. He beckons to Lorraine and she starts to step forward.

"Wait." I grab her arm. "You're not going down there alone, are you?" My voice is starting to get squeaky again.

She frowns. "You can come too, Hunter."

"No, he can't," Briner says. "I don't like him."

"But—" Lorraine starts.

"No," the man says again, shaking his head. "Hunter should stay here."

"Then Lorraine's not going down there without me," I say loudly, trying to get rid of the shrillness in my voice.

Why does the man want to get her alone down there so badly? I think, staring at him, trying to figure it all out. It's obvious that the Amnesia Dust has brought some sort of change over Briner, taking away all the aspects I once feared. Now, with his pointed goatee and black suit, he looks like some little TV villain. And an unconvincing one at that. But when is all this going to wear off? He can't stay like this forever.

"I'm going to go down, Hunter," Lorraine says, breaking into my thoughts. "You can stay and look around for the Glass up here."

"But I don't even know what it looks like," I squeak. "Let me come with you."

My sister glances back towards the man. "It's up to Mr. Briner."

"Who cares what he says! Actually, neither of us should be going down there, anyway."

"Why not?" Briner breaks in, sounding suddenly nervous. "Is there something down there I should know about?"

"Oh, of course not, Mr. Briner," Lorraine tries to reassure him, but he only looks more frightened.

"Why's the boy acting like there is, then?" He glances over his shoulder and down the dark corridor. "If Lorraine doesn't go, I don't go, either. It's scary down there."

Lorraine sighs. "Oh, for heaven's sake—I'll go down myself, then. Mr. Briner, you can stay up here with Hunter. How does that sound? Does that make everyone happy?"

"Sure it does," I answer sarcastically. "Leave me up here with the crazy guy."

"Crazy guy?" Briner repeats. "You are not talking about me, are you?"

"Oh, no, of course not—" Lorraine starts to answer.

"Because I don't appreciate being spoken about like that." The man gives me a hurt, angry look. "You think it's funny to ridicule my position. I did not ask for this to happen to me. I only want it to be put right." He hangs his head as Lorraine pats his shoulder consolingly.

"Oh, yes, that's what we're trying to do now, Mr.

Briner," she says, then she turns towards me. I fold my arms and roll my eyes at her. I'm not feeling quite as sympathetic as my sister is at the moment.

"Come on, Hunter," she mutters anxiously, coming over toward me. "I want to help this man, but I can't do it without your cooperation. If you're going to be so disagreeable about being here alone with him, then you and I can go down the corridor together. How does that sound?"

She gives me a pleading look and I stare back at her. Her idea doesn't sound *too* bad this time, even though I'm not feeling exactly enthusiastic. With a relenting sigh, I turn back to Briner. "Yeah, but will *he* go for it?"

"Oh, I don't know. There's only one way to find out."

She goes back to where he is standing. "Mr. Briner? We have another idea. Hunter and I have decided we will both go down together and you can stay up here in the shop, where it's safe. That's the best way, I think."

Briner bites his lip, looking as tense as I feel.

"Alright," he says finally. "But how long will you two be gone?"

"Oh, not very long," she answers. "Maybe twenty minutes at most. The only problem is, we're not exactly sure what the Glass looks like. Can you remember?"

"Well...like a glass, I suppose."

"A window pane, you mean?" I ask.

"No, it's smaller than that. And..." he squints, "it's

shaped like one of those things, you know...a soup can." He expels his breath and looks towards us expectantly.

I frown, thinking, *a soup can?*

"Oh!" Lorraine says suddenly. "It's shaped like a cylinder!"

"Yes, cylinder, that was the word." The man spreads his hands about a foot apart. "And it's about this long."

"Oh, good," Lorraine says. "We'll be able to find that!"

"Don't be so sure," I mutter into her ear.

"Okay, Mr. Briner," she says, ignoring me. "Now we know what the Glass looks like. Can you tell us where to find it?"

"Down there." He points to the corridor.

"Yes, we already know that," Lorraine says, a little impatiently. "But *where* down there? Where does it lead?"

He shrugs his shoulders hopelessly. "I can't remember."

"Oh well, then. We'll just have to navigate it ourselves, won't we, Hunter?"

I groan in reply and she grabs my arm. "Come on, Hunter. The sooner we get down there, the sooner we can find the Glass."

As we start towards the doorway, Lorraine calls over her shoulder, "We'll be back, Mr. Briner! Just wait right here for us!"

He nods a little miserably after us.

CHAPTER ELEVEN

WHEN FURNITURE ATTACKS

"I hope that guy doesn't cause any trouble while we're gone," I mutter as Lorraine closes the red door behind us.

"Oh, I don't think he will," she replies, pulling me along by the arm. I glance around as we retreat further; despite the eerily light torches, the corridor is dank and cold. The stone floor is descending steadily and I say (shivering slightly), "I wonder how far this place goes down."

Lorraine shrugs as we turn a corner. "I don't know, maybe—" she stops suddenly and I run into her.

"Oh, look!" she exclaims. "A door!"

"Yeah, I noticed that," I answer sarcastically, edging around her to get a better view. The door looks quite a bit like the one we went through a minute ago; small, with red paint peeling off it. Then, before I can say anything else, Lorraine darts forward to open it.

"Ooh." She sticks her head through the doorjamb. "It's a room."

I tiptoe up nervously and peer over her shoulder. The room is small and dark, lit only by a few small candles. The yellow light they cast flickers over two old desks, chairs crowded around them. I glance down at one chair and notice sinister-looking designs carved into the wood. I gulp and look towards Lorraine, but she has already pranced into the room.

"Lorraine, get back here!" I snap.

She frowns at me. "Why should I? We're *supposed* to be looking for the Glass, remember?"

"Yeah, but—"

"Oh, look, here's another door!" She hurries over to the opposite wall, pushing it open and ducking inside. "This must be his bedroom!"

I grimace and scramble after her, wishing she would wait for me before barging into everything. Suddenly, I trip over the clawed leg of a desk and fall flat on my face. As a cloud of dust rises up from the floor, I groan and clutch my elbow. A snicker sounds from above me; I look up. Lorraine is standing over me, shaking her pony-tailed head.

"Oh, Hunter, you goof."

I'm about to answer scathingly, but then I notice something in her hand.

"You've got the Glass!"

"Yep!" Smiling happily, she holds up a small glass cylinder, open at both ends. It glimmers slightly in the dim light. Grinning as well, I get to my feet.

"Well, that's great! Now we can show it to Briner and—ouch!!"

For some reason, I've managed to trip over the desk leg again. Pushing myself up for the second time, I shoot a glance towards the perpetrating desk. I'm starting to get a familiar, suspicious twinge in my chest as I survey it.

"What is it, Hunter?" Lorraine asks, noticing my frown.

"Nothing...I don't know." I pass my hand over my bruised elbow. "But I could have sworn..."

"Sworn what?"

"That—that desk leg just moved!"

Lorraine giggles. "Oh, maybe you're just clumsy, Hunter."

"No, I'm being serious! I—aggghh, it moved again!"

Shrieking in terror, I jump backwards into Lorraine. The desk leg is reaching forward, shaking its clawed fist. One of its drawers has slid open like a mouth.

"*Trespasserss...*" it hisses menacingly, "*Trespasserss...*"

"Oh, no!" Lorraine cries. "We're not trespassers! Mr. Briner sent us here, we—"

The desk lunges forward suddenly, headed straight for us. Yelping, I spin around and start for the door, Lorraine for once following my example. Suddenly, another desk leaps in front of us, blocking our path. I make to veer around it, but from my left a chair lunges forward, butting me hard in the side. I fall to my knees and Lorraine trips right over me. I cover my head protectively with my hands; the chair has started to bash its front legs into me. Just then, I feel a hand grabbing my shirt collar, trying to drag me back up.

"Come on, Hunter, let's go!" my sister shouts into my ear.

"I know, that's what I'm trying to do!" I snarl at her, staggering to my feet and aiming a kick at the attacking chair. It fires back with another head butt, knocking me into Lorraine and sending us both over the top of the desk. We land hard on the other side—right next to the door. Lurching to my feet for the hundredth time tonight, I stumble out into the corridor, dragging Lorraine with me. She spins around, slamming the door shut in the face of the pursuing furniture. We hear a crunching sound of wood on wood as the chairs slam into the door.

"Let's go!" I gasp, and we set off at a run down the corridor together.

"That was a close one," Lorraine pants as our sneakers slap against the wet stone floor. Then she points. "Oh, look, there's the door up ahead!"

Freedom, I think desperately to myself. *We'll both be in the shop with Briner in two seconds so we can give him the Glass and get the heck out of—*

"Wait!" I say aloud, screeching to a halt and turning around. "Do you still have the Glass?"

Lorraine grins, dropping a hand from the stitch in her side to hold it up. "Yes, I still have it! What a miracle, it's not even broken! Not even after all that!"

Sighing heavily, I wipe some sweat off my forehead. "The *real* miracle tonight is that we're still alive. I told you I had a bad feeling about this place, Lorraine. More than the Glass could have been smashed in that room: our heads could have been. What was that guy thinking, having furniture like that?!"

Lorraine shrugs, still panting a little. "Some sort of security measure. And it worked, didn't it?" She grins again, but I don't grin back. Turning around, I start back to the red door, pushing it open. I don't think I'm going to smile again until I get out of this shop.

Briner is sitting at his desk. He jerks around at the sound of the door opening. For a moment, he just stares at me, then at Lorraine.

"What the—" he says confusedly, "who are you two—? Oh, wait, now I remember! Hunter and Lorraine! You're back!" He stands up, the confusion leaving his face and being replaced with a look of relief.

"Yes, we're back," Lorraine answers, pushing around me and going into the shop. I follow her, limping slightly.

"You two took quite a long time," the man says. "I almost forgot about you." He frowns suddenly, noticing our mussed up clothing and faltering steps. "But what's happened to you? What's wrong?"

"Oh, we, ah..." Lorraine glances towards me, "ran into some furniture."

"Oh," Briner replies. "You really should watch where you are going!"

"Don't worry, we will from now on," I mutter darkly. The man turns to me, but is distracted as Lorraine holds the Glass up.

"You have it! The Glass!" He hurries towards her and she gives it to him.

"It was a lot of trouble to find," she remarks, rubbing a bruise on her arm. "I hope you know how to work it, Mr. Briner!"

"Don't worry, I do," he answers, setting the Glass on his desk, right side up. I edge a little closer, curious in spite of myself. How is this man going to call his brother with this? I watch as he taps a finger against his chin, apparently thinking hard.

"Let's see," he mutters. "If I can remember his number..."

Lorraine and I glance at each other over his bent head. Lorraine's eyes are shining. Obviously, she's wondering excitedly about what's going to happen next. I frown. I don't understand how she can still be excited about what's going on in this place. Although I'm no longer frightened (too much of that emotion in one night, I suppose), I still feel miserable. Rubbing my sore arm, I turn my thoughts back to Briner.

"Three..." he is muttering, "or is it four...no, three. Three...two...seven...yes, but what's next? Ah, yes...five, then eight!" He straightens. "Alright, I have the number now! 32758!"

"Oh, good!" Lorraine claps her hands together.
"Now to call it," Briner says, smiling. I watch as he puts one hand on the Glass, turning it three times on the table, then two times the other way, then seven, five, and finally eight times. He straightens up and there's a momentary pause.

I jump as a beam of light suddenly shoots up from the top end of the Glass. All three of us look up where the beam has reflected a large, bright circle on the ceiling. I stare in shock, for the dark silhouette of a man's head has appeared in the yellow circle. It looks a lot like a shadow puppet, the kind I used to make when I was little. Unlike a shadow puppet, however, the silhouette speaks.

"What is it, Artmas?" the voice booms through the little shop. "Why are you calling so late?"

"I need your help, Eugene," Briner answers, rubbing his hands together anxiously.

"With what?"

"With, ah..." he glances toward Lorraine and me, "well, I got myself into a little fix."

"Yes, I assumed *that* much," the head replies, now sounding slightly irritated. "Where are you now, at the shop?"

"Yes."

"So, what's happened? Were you robbed? I told you those wards weren't strong enough—"

"Wards? What are wards?"

The head pauses. "What do mean, 'what are wards'? You know what wards are."

"Ahh..." Briner glances back towards us, obviously at a loss of what to say next.

"Um, excuse me, Mr. Eugene?" Lorraine finally pipes up, recovering for him.

The head starts. "Yes, what? Who is this?"

"Well, I am Lorraine Thomas," she replies, straightening and putting on her most formal English accent, "and this is my young brother, Hunter Thomas. We are Mr. Briner's customers."

"Customers? At this hour? I didn't know you kept the shop open so late, Arty." He shoots this last comment to Briner, who frowns.

"Is it really so late? What time is it, Eugene?"

"Well, it's one in the morning. And you're not sounding quite like yourself. What's really the matter?"

"Oh, perhaps *I* should explain, Mr. Eugene," Lorraine butts in again. "It all started with a shoe—"

"Let's cut to the chase, huh, Lorraine?" I mutter to her. She frowns huffily, but I ignore this and turn back to the head.

"Your brother was hit by Amnesia Dust about twenty minutes ago," I say, wanting to get this over with. "Amnesia Dust he says you created. He can't remember anything and now he needs your help. He was hoping you would know a cure."

"Amnesia Dust?!" the head exclaims. "I don't even want to know how *that* happened!" It pauses. "How did it happen?"

He spilled it," Lorraine answers quickly for me. "On himself."

"On himself, did he?" the head repeats. "That doesn't sound like Artmas. Usually he's not so clumsy. Is that how it happened, Arty?"

Briner shrugs. "I can't remember."

"Of course you don't." The head shakes back and forth. "Well, I think I might have something to help you. I'll be right over. Can you...three wait? There are only three of you there, right?"

"Right," Lorraine answers.

"Okay, then. I'll be right over."

The light in the ceiling is abruptly extinguished as the strangest long-distance conversation of my life ends.

"Oh," Lorraine sighs, turning towards us, "that went well, didn't it?"

"I guess so," I answer. "Eugene didn't sound *too* bad." I glance towards the door. "But I hope he gets here soon. Did you hear what he said? It's already one o'clock! We've been here an hour!"

Lorraine shakes her head, but she's grinning. "Oh, I know. But it was worth it. We're much closer to getting the Shoe now, aren't we?"

"Shoe?" Briner breaks in with his vague voice. "What shoe?"

"The Teleporter," she answers.

"Oh yes, the Teleporter." Briner smiles. "The things people invent these days!"

"Your brother Eugene probably invented it," I say, rubbing my sore arm again.

"Oh, he probably did!" Lorraine exclaims. "Maybe he could make another one! We should ask him when he gets here!"

I frown. "We need to get this problem with Briner resolved first. The Shoe can wait."

"But the Shoe is the whole reason we're here!"

"Yes, I know! It's the reason for this whole stupid situation!" I rub my forehead wearily with both hands.

"Man, I hope this Eugene character gets here quick. I can't wait for—"

Suddenly, there's a loud knocking on the door. Both Briner and I jump, but Lorraine answers sarcastically, "Well, it seems your wish has just been granted, Hunter. That's probably Eugene right now." She starts over to the door.

"You should ask who it is first," I say, my heart starting to pound again. "It might not be him."

"Well, it is," a deep voice calls from outside. "And why are you letting your customers answer the door for you, Artmas?"

"Eugene!" Briner says excitedly, pushing past both me and Lorraine to open it. A black-haired, mustached man strides into the room, looking around. I notice he's wearing a long maroon cape instead of a business suit like his brother. However, it's easy to see they're related.

"Artmas!" He grabs Briner by the shoulders and looks into his eyes. "Well, I can see that he's under the Dust." Then he looks towards us and says, "You two must be Lorraine and Hunter." I notice he speaks with the same slight accent as Briner.

Lorraine curtseys to him, and he grins. "Charmed, I'm sure. You are both from England, I take it?"

"We're not from England," I answer. "Lorraine's accent is fake."

Eugene raises his eyebrows in surprise. "Um, well...fake, but very convincing."

As he turns back around, I let out a small sigh of relief. Unlike his brother, he seems to be friendly enough. I know it's dangerous to trust strangers so quickly, but I think he's safe. I'm not getting any bad vibes from him, at least.

"So you think you can do something for Mr. Briner?" Lorraine asks him.

"Yesss..." he says slowly, walking in a circle around A.T. "But first I'll need to know how much he ingested."

"I don't know," Briner answers automatically.

"Oh, the whole bagful," Lorraine answers.

Eugene looks at her. "The *whole* bagful?! Well, he is showing signs of overdose. But how did this happen?" He shakes his head.

Lorraine and I glance at each other nervously. I know we're thinking the same thing. Should we tell him the truth? I wonder what Eugene will do if he learns how the whole thing actually started. I look back towards him and see that he is staring at us.

"Do you children have *any* way of explaining this?" he asks, tapping a finger against his lips. He doesn't look angry, but seems suspicious. "I can't help but think you two are hiding something."

"Well..." Lorraine rings her hands apologetically. "I suppose I should say...it was a bit...our fault."

"What do you mean—it wasn't our fault!" My voice cracks slightly and I glance towards Briner. His mouth has fallen open and he's gaping at Lorraine.

"*You* did this to me?!" he splutters. "*You* did this to me?! And I thought you two were my friends!"

"We are, Mr. Briner, please understand—"

"No! You tricked me!"

"But Mr. Briner—"

"*SILENCE!*"

The voice rings through the little shop; we all jump and look around at Eugene, who has just shouted the command. His hands are raised, but now that he has our attention, he lowers them.

"Now, let's all just settle down. Lorraine," he points a finger at her, "why don't *you* tell *me* the story, from the beginning. That way I'll be able to know what's going on here." He folds his arms, looking at her.

"Oh, well, um..." she starts off slowly, slightly daunted at being put on the spot. "Well, you see, it began two days ago, when Hunter and I purchased a Teleporter from this shop. The next day, however, our Teleporter was stolen and we never had a chance to use it. So we came back tonight to see if we could purchase another one. Mr. Briner let us in. Then he threatened Hunter with a bag of Amnesia Dust, and tried to force him to take it. Apparently, he thought that Hunter wasn't trustworthy enough to know about the shop.

"Anyway, there was a struggle over the Dust, and it ended up pouring over Mr. Briner. As you can see, he's lost some of his memory. That's why we called you."

"So it *was* your fault!" Briner bursts out in a horrified tone. "I should—"

"Actually, it's your fault, Mr. Briner," I glare at him, but keep myself behind Lorraine just in case. "None of this would have happened if you hadn't decided to throw all that stupid Dust over me."

Briner opens his mouth to retort, but Eugene steps forward. "Alright, alright," he says slightly impatiently. "I think we're a little over the blaming game now."

"Oh, what should we do, Eugene?" Lorraine asks him.

"First," he says, rubbing his chin, "we've got to administer the antidote to Artmas."

"*Now*?" I say. "But won't your brother start to go after me again once he's back to himself?"

"Don't you worry about that." Eugene claps me on the shoulder. "I'll take care of him."

Taking a vial out of his pocket, he turns towards Briner. "Alright. One gulp of the Refreshing Rehabilitator and you'll be good as new, Artmas. Normally, it only takes two drops, but in the case of your overdose..."

Briner snatches the vial, a look of relief on his face. Uncorking it, he throws back his head to take a gulp. I watch nervously as the swallow moves down his throat. I'm definitely not looking forward to having him back to his usual self.

Lowering the vial, Briner shakes his head. "Wheww, quite strong. I can feel it working. Already, I—"

Suddenly, an odd look comes over his face. He steps back for a moment, frowning, then abruptly crashes to the floor.

Chapter Twelve

The Debate

Beside me, Lorraine shrieks, but I'm too stunned to do anything. Is he dead? Is it an allergic reaction to the antidote? I look around quickly towards Eugene.

"What—" I start to say.

Eugene shakes his head. "I should have expected this to happen," he says. "After most patients take the Rehabilitator, they tend to feel a little woozy. And since Artmas ingested so much, he's obviously having a more dramatic reaction." Moving past me, Eugene kneels down beside Briner, propping his head up off the floor.

"Come on, Arty," he mutters, shaking him slightly.

"Oh, I hope he's alright," Lorraine whispers to me.

"I'm sure he will be," I murmur, patting her shoulder. "Our ol' Arty has a habit of bouncing back."

She frowns at me. "Don't be sarcastic, Hunter. You know that if Mr. Briner is seriously hurt, we'll never get the Shoe back."

"Oh, so that's it, is it?" I say snidely. "It's about the Teleporter, not poor Briner." I'm feeling too tense to sound polite. In a few minutes, Briner is going to start remembering some things. Some things about the Dust. And about me.

"Look, he's waking," Eugene calls to us suddenly, and I gulp. Lorraine steps forward curiously. Briner has started to sit up, rubbing his head.

"Oh," he groans. "Damn you, Eugene. Why did you tell me to take such a large gulp?"

Eugene grins, helping Briner to his feet. "Well, it knocked the amnesia out of you, didn't it?"

"Knocked!" Briner snorts, pulling his arm out of Eugene's grip. As he turns to me, I step backward slightly. The sharp, cold look has returned to his pale eyes.

"Well, Mr. Thomas," he says, smoothing down the front of his suit. "You should be feeling exceedingly thankful right now."

"Thankful for what?" I manage to croak out. *That he hasn't killed me yet?*

Briner smiles. "That it was only the Dust I threatened you with. For if it had not been—"

"Now, now," Eugene says, "*You* should be the one to feel so thankful, Artmas."

124

Briner frowns. "And why is that?"

"Well, for one, you've got your memory back!" Eugene raises his eyebrows. "So let's try to be a little civil. They're only children."

"*Children!*" Briner snarls. He turns around to face us with a glare so hard that I step backward again. I'm definitely missing the other A.T.

"Look, just look what they did to me!" he continues angrily.

Eugene puts his arms around his brother's shoulders. "I know, but it's over now. Please, look into your heart to forgive them."

I snort. I doubt the man even *has* a heart to forgive us with. But Lorraine, ever the optimist, steps forward.

"Oh, yes, Mr. Briner, please look into your heart." With her hands clasped in front of her, she shoots him a pleading look. He starts to snarl back at her, then stops and turns away. I hear him mutter something under his breath.

Eugene grins. "What was that, Arty?"

"I said," Briner glowers back at Lorraine, "'Whatever.'"

"I think old Arty has a little soft spot for you!" Still grinning, Eugene nudges Lorraine in the ribs. She blushes and Briner scowls. I scowl too; I doubt the man has a soft spot for anyone, but I don't like anyone saying that about him and my sister.

"So," I break in loudly, "now that Mr. Briner's cured, what are we going to do about the Shoe?"

"The Teleporter, you mean?" Briner shoots me a cold look. "Well, I suppose you two have no choice but to accept the fact that Mrs. Hazelton will keep it."

"What?!" Lorraine bursts out. "Why is that, Mr. Briner?"

"*Because*," (Briner's speaking in a low, slow voice, as if we're stupid), "I no longer have any intention of retrieving it for you."

"But, but..." Lorraine is spluttering and I notice she's lost her accent. "You said—"

"Never mind what I said!" Briner snaps. "I have now decided not to do so. Deal with it."

"Wait a moment, Artmas," Eugene says. "You made these children a promise."

Briner snorts. "I did no such thing."

I'm starting to feel a little sick. Briner's *not* going to go after the Shoe? Does that mean this whole horrible, horrifying night was for *nothing*! Oh, it had better not be!

Before I can even comprehend what I'm doing, I leap in front of Briner. All the rage and fear I've felt for the past two days squeezes into a ball inside my chest, then explodes with such force that Briner jumps backward. "YOU'RE GOING TO GO AFTER THAT FREAKING SHOE!" I roar into his startled face. "I DON'T CARE WHAT YOU HAVE TO DO TO GET IT, JUST GET IT!"

"Now look here, young man—" Briner is trying to recover himself.

"No, you look here!" I growl at him. "You don't know how hard this stuff has been for me!" I start ticking off with my fingers. "First your creepy shop, then Mrs. Hazelton stole our Shoe, *then* we had to break into her house, *then* the cops came, and now I'm grounded! And if Mom and Dad get up in the night and see us gone..." I groan and put my hands against my head.

"The cops came?" Eugene says.

"Oh, Hunter, I didn't know you felt that way," Lorraine says.

Panting, I turn around and fix them both with a glare. Out of the corner of my eye, I see Briner gaping at me. Obviously, he didn't expect my little outburst.

"Mr. Thomas..." he starts to say.

"What?" I snap at him. Truth be told, I didn't expect my little outburst, either. I'm still afraid of the man, but now I'm too angry and exhausted to care.

"What he wanted to say," Eugene has stepped in front of him, "is that he *will* bring back the Teleporter for you. He has thought things over and decided it is best for you children." He turns towards his brother. "Isn't that right, Artmas?"

'Artmas' frowns. He looks from my flushed face, to Lorraine's pale one, then back to Eugene. There is a long silence. Finally, he mutters, "Well, I suppose you all—and

Mr. Thomas—leave me with no choice." Is it my imagination, or is there a smidge of guilt in his face, despite the crotchety tone?

Behind me, I hear Lorraine sigh in relief. "Oh, does that mean you are going to help us?" she says.

"Yes, yes," Briner answers. "And I suppose I might as well get some pay from it. You still have that twenty-three dollars, I take it?"

"What...oh, yes!" She scampers over to where she and I had discarded our parkers an hour earlier. Rifling through a pocket, she pulls out the money and hurries back to Briner. He plucks it out of her hand with a grim smile. "Thank you."

"You're welcome," she says breathlessly. "Are you going to head to Florida now?"

"Florida?" Eugene asks.

"Yes, Florida." Briner rolls his eyes. "That is where the thief, a Mrs. Hazelton, is now."

"Well, that sounds exciting." Eugene grins.

Briner only rolls his eyes again. Putting the money into the inside pocket of his suit, he says unhappily, "I really have no idea how long I will be down there. The shop will be standing idly."

"I could take it over for you," Eugene offers.

"Last time I left the shop to you, you rearranged all the bookshelves. I told you they were in a specific order—"

"Oh, hush," Eugene remonstrates. "I'll do no such thing now; you know I am reliable."

Briner glares. "I suppose I have no choice but to believe that. Very well." With a sigh, he walks across the room and goes behind his desk. After a moment he beckons us. "Lorraine, Mr. Thomas."

We both come forward. I'm feeling more exhausted than ever. Now that I know Briner is actually going to go after the Teleporter, I just want to go back home. What else does he want from us?

"Now," he looks between us, "I shall be leaving shortly. But before I go..." he sits down in his chair and puts his elbows on the desk, "there is something I wish to say."

I shift uneasily from foot to foot. I've got a feeling this next barb will be directed at *me*. Sure enough, he fixes me with his greenish eyes. "Mr. Thomas, I still do not believe you deserve to have use of such a delicate object. And the Teleporter...is delicate. It is meant only for those who *believe* it, *respect* it. You feel none of these things. But alas, I don't have a choice." He continues to study me for a long moment, and I force myself to look back. Finally, he raises his head, nodding to Eugene.

Eugene comes over. "You're ready, Artmas?"

"Yes. I'll go pack. And make sure the children don't touch anything while I'm gone." Shooting a final glare at us, Briner gets to his feet and slips through the door behind his desk.

As soon as he's gone, Lorraine turns to Eugene. "Oh, Mr. ah, Eugene—"

"Just Eugene." He smiles.

"Eugene, then! I want to thank you for...coming out so late...and fixing him. I really appreciate it; and I can't wait to get that Teleporter back!" She shakes his hand appreciatively.

"Absolutely no problem," he answers, then glances at me. "And Hunter?"

"Yeah?" I ask warily. He is giving me a serious look.

"I just want to apologize, on my brother's behalf, for what happened to you tonight. Artmas can be a bit protective about his shop, but he didn't mean any true harm by the Amnesia Dust."

"Sure," I say a little shakily, but I don't think I believe him. Briner had seemed pretty intent on true harm.

A moment later, the devil himself reappears, carrying a suitcase in one hand and a broomstick in the other. He glances around the shop, as if to ascertain nothing befell it in his short absence, then says, "Well, I must be off."

"Well, have a good trip," Eugene says, clapping him on the shoulder. "Do you have the invisibility concoction I mixed?"

When Briner holds it up, Eugene adds, "Excellent!"

"Oh, how long do you think you'll be gone, Mr. Briner?" Lorraine breaks in.

Briner shrugs his shoulders coolly, then looks at the map on his desk. "I really can't say. The tracker indicates that Mrs. Hazelton is still in Florida, but she may move at any time. Eugene, I will contact you as soon as I can. You can tell the children my progress."

Eugene nods. Briner furls the map back up, stows it in his suitcase and walks towards the door. We all follow him, Lorraine huffing nervously. My heart is starting to beat quickly. *He's going, he's finally going*! I'm faint with relief.

Briner starts to uncork the invisibility concoction when Lorraine grabs his arm. "You'll be careful, won't you, Mr. Briner?"

Briner smirks at her. "I shall be. But I daresay your concern is more for the Shoe than I."

"Well, they are both important." She blushes, stepping back for Eugene to shake his brother's hand. Then Briner takes a gulp of the invisibility concoction and he and the broom disappear completely from sight. I jump, but manage to contain a gasp. For the first time, I realize that this situation is crazy, but very *real*. The thought frightens me. I barely notice Lorraine's squeal of delight, or the door opening and shutting.

"Well, that's it, then," Eugene says, turning around. "Why don't we—Hunter, what's wrong? You look a little pale."

"What? Oh, nothing," I croak. "I'm fine. It's just a little late."

"Hmm." Eugene casts me an unconvinced look before looking down at his watch. "Well, it *is* quite late! Nearly 2:00. You two ought to be getting back home."

"Oh, when will you contact us, Eugene?" Lorraine asks him.

"As soon as I hear news from Artmas," he answers. "I suppose the best way would be for me to write you. I don't have a phone."

I think back on the Glass. Lorraine is saying, "Alright, I'll give you our address. Have you got a pen?"

"Whoa, whoa, hold on a minute." I grab her arm. "There's no reason to give out our address."

"Well, then how is he going to write us?" she asks sarcastically. "Send us a letter by magic?"

"I'm sure he'll be able to do that," I sneer at her. "He is a magician, remember?"

"Actually," Eugene breaks in calmly, "you are referring to those silly fellows who have milk disappear into a top hat at parties. I am a wizard."

"See, even better."

Lorraine glowers, pulling her arm from my grip. "Fine. But he is *not* a thief, Hunter. I feel perfectly fine giving him our address."

"Well, I don't."

Eugene laughs suddenly, startling us both. He's regarding me, but he doesn't seem angry.

"My brother was rather right about you, wasn't he?"

"What's that supposed to mean?" I ask cagily.

"I think you already know." He smiles at me. "But don't worry, I don't need your address. There *are* other methods of communication." Picking Briner's Glass off the desk, he continues. "You can simply borrow this of Arty's; I don't think he'll mind. Do you both know how to use it?"

Lorraine and I nod.

"Good. So here's my number..." He scribbles something on a piece of paper and hands it to Lorraine, along with the Glass. "Now remember, the Glass is very fragile. You have to be careful with it."

"Oh, we will," she promises.

"Good." Eugene glances at his watch again. "Now you two had better *really* be going. I'll call as soon as I can."

"Thank you," Lorraine says, then nudges me in the ribs.

"Oh...yeah, thanks," I mutter.

"Sure thing," Eugene replies, "I'll see you to the door, shall I?"

Lorraine and I pick up our parkas and put them on. Eugene gives them a puzzled look, but seems to decide not to say anything. He leads us to the door. Goodbyes exchanged, Eugene wishes us good luck, then we are outside in the night air.

CHAPTER THIRTEEN

CAUGHT IN THE ACT

My legs begin to shake slightly as we start down Tuttle Road. My head is aching and my body feels strangely light, despite the thick parka. Beside me, Lorraine says brightly, "Well, wasn't that an adventure!"

"I feel like I'm going to throw up," I mumble.

"Oh, Hunter," she throws her arms around me, "I'm so glad you came! It wouldn't have been the same without you."

"Humph," I say.

"Just think," she continues, "we're about to get our Teleporter back!"

"We don't have it yet," I remind her. "And we might *never* have it. That guy's not too trustworthy, is he?"

Lorraine puts her hands on her hips. "Mr. Briner is certainly trustworthy! Stop being so pessimistic, Hunter."

"I'm not being pessimistic, I'm being realistic." I sigh and put my hand against my head. "I'm tired of arguing, Lorraine. Can we just be quiet for awhile?"

"Fine," she snaps huffily. We continue for a few minutes in silence. Lorraine opens her mouth once or twice, as if about to say something, then decides against it.

Good, I think to myself. *Finally some relief.*

Before I know it, we're sneaking down the alleyway behind our street. It seems to have taken less time to leave Monty's than to get to it. My heart starts to pound a little harder as we near our house. Are Mom and Dad still asleep? Or did they wake up to notice two beds were conspicuously empty?

I swallow, hoping it's the former. Lorraine puts her finger to her lips and we scramble over our fence together, landing with a thud in the backyard. I shoot a nervous glance towards the house, but everything's still and silent. Lorraine's already scurrying towards my window and I follow after her. It's still open from when we left it, so I breathe a sigh of relief. That probably means Mom and Dad were asleep this whole time.

"Boost me up," Lorraine whispers in my ear.

With a grunt, I manage to bend down, even in my parka, and boost her over the window sill. She turns around to help me up. I start to reach for her hand, then stop.

"Oh, what is it, Hunter?" she whispers.

"I-I don't know," I stammer, "I just thought I heard—"

"*WHAT IN THE HELL ARE YOU DOING?*"

Dad has just burst into my room. A flashlight beam hits Lorraine directly in the face. Without thinking, I duck down, flattening myself against the wall. Dad hasn't seen me yet, and I'm not exactly ready to give him an opportunity to do so. Above me, I hear Lorraine stammer, "Oh, uh, I was just opening the window...getting a little fresh air—"

"Fresh air? *Fresh* air?" I hear Dad stomp across the room. On my elbows and knees, I crawl out from under the window. I'm almost around the side of the house when Dad snarls, "In Hunter's room? Getting fresh air in Hunter's— wait a minute! Where's Hunter?"

I freeze, sweat pouring down my face. The collar of my parka feels like it's tightening dangerously. I barely hear Lorraine's answer: "Oh well, I don't know, maybe he went..."

"Maybe he went where? Is Hunter outside?"

When Dad is two seconds from sticking his head out the window, I lunge around the side of the house. Scrambling to my feet, I tear off my parka. A sort of desperate idea has lodged into my head. Maybe, just maybe, I can get back inside, before Dad even finds I went out. But *only* if I act quickly. My heart pounding, I tear towards Lorraine's bedroom window and shove it open. With a groan, I boost myself over the edge and topple inside as quietly as I can. I can still hear Dad and Lorraine arguing in the next room. Then Mom's voice joins them. I jump to my feet and start towards the door. *I'm in, I'm in...now all I have to do is convince them I never—*

"OWW! Son of a—"

I trip over a carton of books on Lorraine's floor and feel my head slam into her bedpost. Sparks flash in front of my eyes. Groaning, I sink to the floor. A moment later, the door flies open. Dad, Mom, and Lorraine all burst in. I look up at them blearily from my position on the carpet.

"Hi, guys."

"Hunter, what happened?" Mom gasps.

"Hunter..." Dad growls. He grabs me by the scruff of my neck and pulls me up, but I only sink on top of Lorraine's bed. For some reason, the room seems to be spinning.

"Hunter, what happened?" Mom says again. She's leaning over me, her worried, concerned face swimming in and out of my vision.

"Nothing, I just hit my head," I mutter. "I think I'll go back to bed now." Lorraine's quilt seems very soft and inviting underneath my sore body. Then Dad's larger, angrier face appears in front of me.

"Not just yet, mister," he says. "You have some explaining to do."

"Explaining about what?" I mumble. I'm not feigning innocence; I really can't remember. My head is hurting so badly I can't recall much of anything.

But before Dad can answer, Mom grabs his arm. "Wait a minute, Daniel. Look at that *lump!*" She stares, almost frightened, at my forehead. "Come on into the kitchen, Hunter. I need to get something for your head."

I get up to follow her. My head is throbbing with every step. Dad doesn't help, breathing down my neck as we walk. Lorraine follows behind us.

"You *are* going to explain what's going on, Hunter," he reminds me as Mom ushers me into a seat and presses an ice pack against my head. I wince at the coldness and the dizziness begins to leave me.

Beside me, I hear Lorraine say, "I can explain, Daddy."

"Well," he puts his hands on his hips, "Let's hear it, then."

"Okay then." She tugs at the collar of her parka. She doesn't sound so English anymore. "I know this all looks bad, Daddy—"

"You bet it does."

"—but I have a perfectly reasonable explanation."

I look up at her, startled. She does? I'm glad Lorraine's taking over for me, but I can't help but worry about what she's going to say next.

She drops her hand from her collar and straightens up. She's looking directly into Dad's eyes. My feeling of foreboding increases. "Hunter...and I decided to switch rooms. You know, me sleep in his and he sleep in mine. We thought it would create...a little diversity. Because we're grounded and all..."

Diversity?! I glance quickly at Dad from under my ice pack. His upper lip is curling like he's about to snarl at her, but he remains silent. My heart drops even further as she continues, apparently gathering steam.

"—And I thought I'd wear my parka because it sometimes gets cold in Hunter's room, but then I got kind of hot in it, so I opened the window—"

"Oh, that's good, very good," Dad interrupts sarcastically. "Even better than that crackpot story you gave the cops. But how exactly did Hunter hit his head? He wasn't used to your bed, so he slid off it? And why is he all dressed? Forgot his pajamas?"

"Um, well, the thing about that is—"

"You know what, Lorraine, I don't think I want to hear anymore." Dad turns away suddenly, as if he's too angry to look at us. "Just...just go to your rooms. I need to decide about your punishments."

I stare at his back, where he's leaning against the counter. Is that all?

"I thought I told you to get to your rooms!" he repeats loudly.

"*Please* go to your rooms," Mom corrects for him, putting her hand on his shoulder.

"Okay," Lorraine squeaks, hurrying off. Feeling dazed, I slide off the chair and follow her. Mom gives me a concerned look. "Hunter, are you sure—"

"I'm fine," I mutter quickly. All I want to do right now is get to my room. Stumbling through the door, I flop down on my bed. The window is still open, but I'm too exhausted and achy to get up and close it. "Forget it," I mumble aloud as I turn over.

My last coherent thought, *What a night!*

Chapter fourteen

A Conversation with Eugene

I wake up the next morning not feeling any happier than I did falling asleep. Dad comes in before leaving for work and informs me that the grounding is now on for several weeks, but if I give him any problems, he will gladly extend it.

I spend the next four hours pacing back and forth across my room, thoughts spinning around in my head. Where is Mrs. Hazelton? Is she still in Florida? Does she have the Shoe with her? Has Briner found her yet? And what about Eugene? Lorraine has the Glass in her room, so I can't know if he has contacted us.

I flop down on my bed, rubbing my temples. So many questions, so few answers. "Who knew one little Shoe could cause so much trouble," I say aloud. And on top of all this, the police are starting their search for Mrs. Hazelton today! *Not that they'll find anything*, I think to myself, rolling off my bed and peering through the blinds of my window. I can't see the street, but my window looks directly at the Hazelton's house. It's very quiet over there, and I wonder where Marty is.

Just then, I hear a knock on my door and my heart jumps slightly. "Come in," I answer.

It's Mom. She looks almost as nervous as I'm feeling. "Hi, honey," she says. "How is your head feeling?"

"Better than last night," I answer, forcing a smile. The lump on my forehead still aches, but I can touch it now without having my eyes water.

"Good," she replies, picking up the now-limp ice pack off my pillow. "I just want you to know that I'm going out for an eye-doctor's appointment, and you're not to leave anywhere while I'm gone."

"I know *that*," I say. "I'm grounded, remember?"

"Yes, you are." Now it's her turn to force a smile. Then she adds, "And just to let you know, the police are outside—"

"They haven't found Mrs. Hazelton yet?" I ask, even though I know the answer.

Mom shakes her head sadly. "Not yet. I'm hoping...well, Mrs. Hazelton was a nice lady."

"She was," I agree. For some reason, I feel a sudden pang of guilt.

Mom, not noticing this, glances at her watch. "Well, I've got to go, honey. I'll be back in an hour or two. Remember, don't give Daddy another excuse to make your groundings longer."

"I'll try, but I don't know if I can," I mutter under my breath, thinking of Lorraine.

"What was that, honey?"

"I said I won't," I answer loudly. I feel a strong relief after Mom leaves. But only a few minutes after I hear her car back out of the driveway, my door opens again.

"What is it, Lorraine?" I groan. She's got an intense look on her face. If she asks me to sneak out again, I'm going to kick her in the shins.

"Nothing, *Hunter*," she replies, rolling her eyes. "I just wanted to know if you want to go into the living room. You can see the cops outside."

"What are they doing?" I ask.

"Talking to Ms. Phelps," she answers. Ms. Phelps is our other next door neighbor. "Come on."

Now curious, I follow her out of the room. She gets up on the couch in our living room and pulls up the blinds.

"Don't be so conspicuous," I hiss, crawling up beside her and nudging her in the ribs.

"Oh, hush," she says. "They can't see us."

I peer through the window with her. We're looking directly out on to Ms. Phelps' front porch. I see Ms. Phelps' head poking out her front door. She's talking to Officer Jim

Meyers, who has his thumbs hooked into his belt. Ryan Wilson is hanging behind him. My heart jumps a little at the sight of them. Suddenly, Ms. Phelps gestures for them to come inside, and they follow her. For a moment, I see all three of their silhouettes through her kitchen window, then they move into a different room.

"Damn it," Lorraine mutters beside me.

"What do you think Ms. Phelps is going to tell them?" I ask her, leaning back on my heels.

Lorraine shrugs. "Oh, I don't know. Ms. Phelps is rather friends with Mrs. Hazelton, isn't she?"

"You could say that," I answer. I used to see her having tea a few times at Ms. Phelps'.

Lorraine rubs her lip musingly. "I wonder why Mrs. Hazelton didn't take Ms. Phelps with her when she tried out the Teleporter?"

"Maybe she wanted to try it out by herself the first time," I answer. Then I go back to the cops. "Say, you don't think they're going to stop at our house next, do you?"

"Who?"

"Wilson and Meyers!"

"Oh, I hope not," she says. "Anyway, our parents aren't home."

"What's that got to do with anything?"

"Oh, I don't know..."

"Man, but they might try to talk to us again. You know, if Mrs. Hazelton doesn't show up for awhile."

She bites her lip. "Well, we'll just have to hope that Artmas finds her soon."

"Artmas?" I sneer. "He's 'Artmas' to you now?"

"Oh, shut up." Lorraine pulls back the blinds again. After a moment she says, "Look, they're coming back out!"

I quickly look through the blinds. Meyers is walking down the porch. Wilson gives one last wave to Ms. Phelps before following after him. Lorraine and I both move to a more convenient window as the cops start walking down the sidewalk, away from their squad car. My chest tightens as they near our house, but they pass it. They also pass the Hazelton's. The house on the other side of the Hazelton's is empty, so they turn back and go across the street. We watch them knock on the Williamson's door, but there seems to be no answer.

"It looks like they're checking out all the houses on our block," I say. "To see if anyone saw anything suspicious from yesterday."

"Oh, do you think anyone saw anything?" Lorraine asks, as the cops move down to the Yung family's door.

"You mean a lady disappearing into thin air clutching a shoe?" I roll my eyes. "I doubt anyone saw that. But if they did, they probably wouldn't tell the police."

"Oh, why not?"

I raise my eyebrows disbelievingly. "Because the whole story sounds crazy, that's why! The cops would think they were pulling a prank. Or throw them in the loony bin."

Lorraine sighs. "Oh, I guess you're right. Too bad nobody would believe our story."

"Actually, you should be glad nobody would believe it. Or else they would all be clamoring to use our shoe."

I push myself away from the window and go into the kitchen to get a drink. Lorraine follows me, biting her lip thoughtfully.

"You know, I've been giving a lot of thought to what we'll do after we get the Shoe back."

"I wouldn't start thinking about that just yet," I reply. "What if we never get the Shoe back? It *is* a possibility." Talking about the Teleporter still makes me nervous. I'm not too sure about the object, even now.

I remember Briner's glittering, greenish eyes, and shudder.

"Oh, I trust Mr. Briner," Lorraine says simply. She goes back into the living room and looks through the window. "Well, the squad car is gone. The police must have left."

"They'll be back," I reply wisely.

Lorraine snaps the blinds shut and straightens up. "I suppose now would be a good time to call Eugene, Hunter. Mom and Daddy aren't here to hear us. Come on." She starts up to her room and I follow her, feeling a little nervous again.

"Has he tried to call you yet?"

"No, not yet."

"He must be busy," I say. "Taking over the shop and everything."

Lorraine starts rummaging through her closet.

"I doubt he's got anything to tell us," I add. "Briner's probably not even in Florida yet."

She ignores me, pulling the Glass out from underneath a sweater and holding it up.

"There," she declares. "And I remember his number..." She hurries over to me and sets the Glass upright on her dresser. It glimmers slightly in the light. I watch with bated breath as she starts turning it the same way Briner did last night. "3...2...7...5...8!"

A beam of light comes shooting out of the glass and hits the ceiling. The now familiar silhouette of Eugene's head appears in it.

"Let me guess," his voice booms, "Hunter and Lorraine?"

It's still very strange to be watching this. Beside me, Lorraine squeals, "Oh yes, it's us, Eugene."

"So what do you need?" he asks. "I'm at the shop right now."

"Are there any customers with you?" she asks.

He shakes his dark head. "No, not yet."

I clear my throat, wanting to speed up the conversation. "Have you heard back from your brother yet, Eugene?" I ask him.

"I have actually," he says. "Just this morning. Apparently, Artmas isn't on the route to Florida any longer."

"Oh, why not?" Lorraine asks.

"Because Mrs. Hazleton isn't there," Eugene answers. "She Teleported herself to another location a few hours ago. San Francisco, California, to be exact."

"California," I groan. "That's even farther than Florida."

"Arty will get there," Eugene reassures us.

"How exactly have you been talking to Artmas?" Lorraine asks. "Does he have a Glass, too?"

"No, Glasses are too fragile to take on journeys." Eugene replies. "He's been sending me memos."

"Memos?" I say curiously.

"Little slips of paper. Artmas sends them through the air and they land on my desk here at the shop only minutes later."

"By magic," Lorraine breaths beside me.

"Exactly," Eugene says. "The only problem with memos is that you can't communicate a lot with them. They're too small for more than a few sentences."

"Oh, I wish I could see one," Lorraine says wistfully.

"Well, you can," Eugene replies. "Come over to the shop."

"Oh, we can't." Lorraine blushes.

"Why not?"

"Because we're grounded," I inform him, feeling suddenly thankful for this.

"Grounded; what does that mean?"

"It means we're not allowed to go anywhere out of the house," I say. "At least not for a couple weeks." Lorraine shakes her head sadly beside me.

"I still don't get it," Eugene says. "Why are you being grounded?"

"As punishment," I answer. "Our parents gave it to us." I wonder what else I should tell him. Nothing about our little break in, at least.

"Well, that sounds pretty—Oh wait, I've got a customer! I've got to go. You two will call me back, won't you?"

"What time would be best?" Lorraine asks.

"Tomorrow morning, I'd say. I might have some more information for you then."

"Oh, okay. Thank you, Eugene."

"Sure thing," he replies, and his head disappears from sight. The light on the ceiling disappears a moment later.

"Well, that didn't tell us very much," I say, sitting down on Lorraine's bed.

"Yes, but we know where Mrs. Hazelton is now, don't we?" Lorraine says grimly. She picks up the Glass and heads towards her closet with it. "In California, enjoying the surf and sun. Not for long, though, not for long."

Chapter fifteen

To Believe or not to Believe

Mom returns from her doctor's appointment about an hour later. The first thing she does is peek in our rooms. To check and make sure we haven't tried to escape again, I suppose bitterly. Dad comes back from work a little while later. Like Mom, he looks into our rooms, but he gives me a glare rather than a sad smile. After I hear his footsteps pad down the hallway, I roll over in bed and stare at my window.

The blinds are closed, but I get up to open them. Early evening light streams into my room. I stare at Marty Hazelton's house from my window, wondering what he's doing. How he's feeling. Does he miss his wife? Lord knows they didn't get along while they were together, but I suppose that doesn't mean they didn't love each other. I smirk to myself, thinking—*well, look at Dad and me. We never get along, but we're family. We love each other.* "At least I think we love each other," I say aloud, resting my arms against the window sill. I stare outside for some minutes, lost in thought. Then, something suddenly catches my eye.

A patrol car is pulling into the Hazelton's drive. The car's ignition cuts off; the familiar forms of Meyers and Wilson climb out. My heart speeds up. Do they have news about Mrs. Hazelton? It seems unlikely, but you never know...I hold my breath and unlatch my window, pulling it up halfway. I press my nose against the glass, watching them as they walk up to the porch. They disappear from my range of vision, but I hear them ring Mr. Hazelton's doorbell. A moment later, Mr. Hazelton himself answers.

"You wanted to see us, sir?" I hear Meyers say.

"Yeah, yeah," Mr. Hazelton answers. His voice sounds hoarse. "I think I've got something to tell you about this case."

Their voices lower for a moment, then I hear the front door close. *They must have gone inside,* I think to myself. My palms are sweating slightly, but I shiver. What news does Mr. Hazelton have about the case? I've got the strange feeling that it's not anything good. I want to tell Lorraine, but I'm afraid to leave my room.

I start to pace up and down. I hear Mom and Dad talking to each other in the kitchen. A sudden rashness seizes me, and I walk quickly to my door and open it. Sneaking on my hands and knees, I go across the hall into Lorraine's room. Lorraine is sitting on her bed, reading a book.

"The cops are here," I tell her after closing the door.

She puts her book down. "Here?"

"At Marty Hazelton's. I heard him talking to them. He told them he knows something about his wife's disappearance."

Her eyes widen slightly. "Oh, do you think it might be about the Shoe?"

"I hope not," I answer. "I can't see how. Unless..."

"Unless what?"

"Maybe Mr. Hazleton did see Esther with the Shoe," I say slowly. "Maybe he even saw her Teleport herself. He just didn't tell the police, because the story sounds so crazy. But now that his wife has been gone this long, he might have told them."

"The police will never believe it," Lorraine says, convinced.

"Yeah," I say, "but it might make it harder for us if we get the Shoe. Marty might see us with it and—"

Suddenly, there's a knock at our house's front door. My heart jumps up in my chest and I spin around. "Oh God, that must be them!"

"Who?"

"The cops!" I hiss. I dart to Lorraine's door and open it. I hear voices drifting from the front of the house. Dad's voice, and an unpleasantly familiar one...(I gulp). Officer Jim Meyers.

Lorraine hops off her bed and comes up behind me. "You're right, it is them!"

Just then, Dad's voice calls, "Hunter, Lorraine, could you kids come here a minute?"

Lorraine and I exchange glances of dread. Then Lorraine calls, "Coming, Daddy!" She pushes me out the door, whispering, "Go on, Hunter. The quicker we get this over, the better."

I try to keep my knees from shaking as we walk down the hallway. The living room slowly comes into view. There are several people gathered in it. Dad, Mom, Officer Meyers and Wilson, and (double gulp!) Marty Hazelton.

Marty glares at me out of beady eyes. I definitely didn't expect him to be here.

"Oh, Daddy, what's going on?" Lorraine says beside me. Her eyes are wide and innocent, as if she can't imagine *why* local law enforcement would be here.

"Why don't you and your brother sit down, Lorraine?" Meyers says casually, his thumbs hooked in his belt. Relieved, I sink into a seat. My legs had felt as if they weren't going to hold up much longer. Lorraine sits down beside me; the officers and my parents file suit. Marty, however, remains standing.

"Kids," Officer Meyers says, looking between us, "Mr. Hazelton has just brought something to our recent attention."

"What's that?" I choke, gripping my seat cushion. Dad notes my reaction with suspicion, but Meyers answers in the same calm voice.

"Mr. Hazleton claims he witnessed you two sneaking out of your house late last night."

Whoa, Meyers doesn't beat around the bush, does he?! I think to myself, sitting back in my seat. But I force my face to look calm; Dad's still watching.

Meyers continues, "He admits this made him suspicious; after all, you two had been caught entering his own home yesterday. And then his wife disappeared...and she hasn't been found yet—"

"But we didn't have anything to do—" Lorraine breaks in.

Meyers raises a hand. "Not saying you did, not saying you did at all. But we do—" he glances sidelong at Mr. Hazelton, "have an interesting set of circumstances here."

I feel sick. No matter what Meyers said to the contrary, I've got a feeling he thinks Lorraine and I have a bigger part in the Hazelton scandal.

For the first time, Ryan Wilson speaks up. "We're just trying to clear things up, guys. I mean, a woman's missing...we've got to cover everything."

"Hunter and I have nothing to do with Mrs. Hazelton's disappearance." Lorraine says, staring Wilson straight in the eye.

"Of course they don't," Mom speaks up. "Why should they?"

"We're not blaming—" Wilson replies hastily.

"Like hell you aren't!" Mr. Hazelton shouts, startling us all. He whirls toward Lorraine. "Admit it, girl! You're guilty! What have you done with my wife?!"

Lorraine freezes in her seat, shocked. I clutch my chest, trying to keep myself from having a heart attack. Dad and Wilson stand up, trying to calm Mr. Hazelton down, but Jim Meyers' voice rises above them all. "Let's have order here, people!"

Everyone freezes and stops talking. Dad and Wilson have their hands on Mr. Hazelton's shoulders. He's panting heavily, but doesn't take his eyes off Lorraine's. Mom's sitting stunned on the couch, looking as if a bomb went off in front of her face. Suddenly, Lorraine leaps to her feet. I've never seen her look so English.

"How dare you presume such a thing, you mad man!" she shouts. "Hunter and I are innocent!"

"Like hell..." Mr. Hazelton gasps.

Dad tightens his grip on the man's shoulders. "Marty, why don't you sit down before you start throwing out accusations against my children again, okay?"

Reluctantly, Mr. Hazelton allows himself to be steered into the Lazy-Boy. "I *still* want to know where my wife is," he says loudly.

Lorraine gives him a cold look. "Hunter and I do not know where she is."

Suddenly, a guilty feeling rips through my chest. I long to shout out the truth, but know such a thing would be impossible.

"Why don't you sit down again, Lorraine," Meyers says in a quiet voice. "You too, Wilson."

Wilson grins awkwardly. "Haven't got a chair, chief. Marty—" he gestures to where Mr. Hazelton is hunched over in the Lazy-Boy.

"Oh, for God's sake..." Meyers mutters.

Mom shoots off the couch, as if she has only been waiting for an excuse to leave the room. "I'll get an extra chair," she gasps, hurrying away. When she appears again and we all get settled, Meyers takes his yellow notepad out of a pocket and sets it on his lap.

"Hunter, Lorraine," he says in a firm voice. "We are not saying that you are the cause of Mrs. Hazelton's disappearance. But we all can't help but feel you are hiding something from us."

If it's possible, I feel even sicker. Meyers leans forward in his chair, his voice suddenly soft. "Go on kids, whatever it is, you can tell us. Don't be afraid."

"There's nothing to tell," Lorraine answers.

"Hunter?" Meyers turns towards me.

"There's nothing to tell," I·repeat, squeaking.

"Kids, do you know what it's called when you don't give a police officer information that he might need for a case?" He pauses. "Obstruction of justice."

I try to keep my face perfectly innocent. Lorraine bursts out, "But we're not obstructing—"

Meyers changes tactics so fast my head spins. "What were you two kids doing out last night?"

Lorraine's mouth is still open but no sound comes out.

"Were you going to find Mrs. Hazelton?" Wilson asks.

"No, we weren't," I answer firmly, finally having something truthful to say.

"Sneaking out to see a friend?" Wilson guesses again.

"No," I answer.

"Then what, going out for a midnight walk?" His voice is starting to become sarcastic.

"We were going to our tree house," Lorraine says suddenly. I turn to her. *Huh?*

"Tree house?" Meyers says.

"Oh yes," Lorraine says. "Hunter and I have a tree house out in the woods not very far away."

I frown. There's a small stretch of woods at the end of our neighborhood, but Lorraine and I certainly don't have a tree house out there. Where is she going with this?

"I don't remember you and Hunter ever having a tree house out there," Dad speaks up suspiciously.

Lorraine blushes. "Oh, my friend Mary's older brother built it a few years ago. Hunter and I have just started using it."

"What do you use it for?" Meyers asks.

"We like to go out there and read," Lorraine answers. "Or talk."

"But why were you there last night?" Wilson asks. He is gazing at us intently. "Did you think Mrs. Hazelton would be there?"

"Why *would* she be there?" I ask, confused. Do the police actually think we're keeping Marty Hazelton's wife captive or something?

"So she *wasn't* there?" Wilson says, his eyes darting between us.

"No, of course not," Lorraine answers.

Wilson looks as if he's about to say something else, but then Meyers nudges him in the ribs, rolling his eyes. "Okay," Meyers says, "we've established the fact that Mrs. Hazelton wasn't in your secret hideout when you got there. But why did you go there?"

"We just...thought...well, it would be an adventure out late at night." Lorraine looks almost apologetic. "Didn't you ever sneak out of the house when you were a boy, Mr. Meyers?"

Meyers' mustache twitches, but I can't tell if he's amused or angry. "We're not talking about me, Miss Lorraine."

"Oh, for God's sake," Mr. Hazelton breaks in, frustrated. "These kids are obviously hiding something! *Make* them tell us what they know!"

"Have you ever thought that maybe your wife just left because she's tired of your attitude?" Lorraine snaps at him. There's a sudden silence in the room. Marty stiffens in his chair. "M-my wife would never leave—" he splutters.

"Wait, wait, hold on a minute." Meyers holds up a hand. "Where's all this coming from?"

Mom and Dad exchange a knowing look. Meyers catches this. "Mr. and Mrs. Thomas, do *you* know something we don't?"

Dad sighs heavily. "Marty and Esther...well, they had their little spats, like any other couple...only a few more than most..."

"I see," Meyers says, his eyes sharp. "So you would describe them as an unhappy couple?"

"Ah, not unhappy," Dad answers, though his voice isn't entirely convincing. He glances sidelong at Mr. Hazelton. "They *did* have arguments, but..."

"But they seemed to get over them," Mom adds, as if unwilling to gossip.

"I see..." Meyers says, very slowly. "So no indication that Esther would feel the need to leave her husband?"

"I don't think so," Dad says. "But I mean—"

"Esther would *never* leave me," Mr. Hazelton breaks in vehemently. He seems to have gotten over his shock. "Never."

"So no big argument a week before? No change in Esther's behavior?" Meyers asks him.

"No, she was the exact same as usual. And don't you think she would have said something a little different to me before she left?" He snorts, his voice rising. "'Goodbye, dear, I'm going out for a little while.' She tells me the same thing when she goes out shopping! She didn't leave, she was *kidnapped*! And these kids have got something do with it!" He points his finger wildly at us. His eyes are bulging.

"Please, Mr. Hazelton, don't accuse our children," Mom says firmly. "They would never do anything to harm your wife."

Mr. Hazelton looks as if he's about to shout something else, but then Dad puts his arms around Mom's shoulders. "She's right, that's enough, Marty. I mean, I know you're upset right now—"

"Damn right I'm upset!"

"Hey, I thought I said order!" Meyers commands. "Now everyone settle down!"

Mr. Hazelton clenches his jaw shut, folding his arms across his chest. For a moment, we all glare at each other.

Then he says, "Now what, Officer? How are you going to find my wife?"

"We're doing the best we can, sir," Wilson replies from where he's sitting by the TV. "What about your notes, Chief?" He glances hopefully at Meyers.

Meyers flips a few pages of his yellow notepad. "Well, let's see," he mutters, starting to scribble for a few minutes. Then he says, "What we should do now is read out all the facts we've got on this case. This whole thing is getting confusing enough as it is...well, we need to start reviewing everything. Wilson?" He hands the notepad out to Wilson, who grabs it eagerly.

"Well, let's see." Wilson clears his throat. "At approximately 10:00 yesterday morning, Mrs. Hazelton left her house, with a statement to her husband that she would return. At..." he leans toward Meyers. "What's that word? I can't read your handwriting too well."

"Approximately," Meyers grumbles.

"Ah, yes. At approximately 10:10, her husband woke up to find Hunter and Lorraine Thomas in his living room. He overheard them speaking about a..."

"Shoe."

"...A shoe of some sort. He then proceeded to contact the police. When the police arrived, Hunter and Lorraine Thomas claimed that Mrs. Hazelton had invited them to enter the house without her..."

"Presence."

"...Presence, to retrieve a pack of playing cards. Apparently, the two children had met Mrs. Hazelton on the sidewalk while she was walking to the bus stop. That evening, it was noted that Mrs. Hazelton had not returned. This morning, neighbors and bus drivers were questioned. All claimed that they had *not* seen Mrs. Hazelton the day of her..."

"Disappearance."

"...Disappearance. This evening, the police were again contacted by Mr. Hazelton. Hazelton stated he had seen the Thomas children sneaking out of their home late last night. When questioned, the Thomas children claimed they had gone to visit a tree house, which was located in a woods not far from their home." Wilson takes a deep breath, looking up. "Is that it, Chief?"

"That's it," Meyers mutters.

I sink down in my seat. Hearing all the facts laid out like that is making my head spin. *I can't believe it's only been two days since school let out!* I think to myself, groaning inwardly.

"Doesn't sound like a lot," Mr. Hazelton says, his arms still folded across his chest.

"You're right, it's not a lot," Meyers answers. He takes his notepad from Wilson and stands up. "I don't think there's anything else we can do here today. Except—" he glances at Lorraine and me, "I'd like to see the kid's tree house, if I can."

"Certainly, Officer," Dad says.

I glance at Lorraine. *Is there even a tree house?* I wonder worriedly. Her face tells me nothing.

"Are you officers leaving now?" Mom asks.

Meyers nods.

"Hey, wait!" Mr. Hazelton bursts out. "What about the kids? Don't you need to question them some more?"

Meyers laughs gruffly. "Maybe later, sir. We'll see."

Chapter Sixteen

The Return of Briner

The tree house expedition didn't go as bad as it could have. Lorraine and I were driven over there by Wilson and Meyers. I had slid down in my seat as low as I could go, not wanting anyone to see my face peeking out the window of a patrol car. When we got to the strip of woods, I was extremely relieved to see a weathered tree house sitting up in an oak tree. The cops had taken a look around, made general comments, then drove us back.

It's the next morning after an uneasy night. I've been plagued with nightmares about being thrown into a jail cell with A.T. Briner and Marty Hazelton. Crawling out of bed, I go to the window, parting the blinds to look out. The Hazelton's house is silent. Just then, there's a knock on the door and Mom enters, carrying a plate of waffles.

"Have they found Mrs. Hazelton yet?" I ask, before she can even say anything.

"No, sorry, honey." She shakes her head. "I know these past couple days have been hard for you..." she sets the waffle plate down to give me a hug, "but I think they'll find Esther."

"I hope so," I mutter into her shoulder.

Mom pulls back and looks me in the eye. "And just so you know, neither I *nor* your father think you had anything to do with her missing. You're good kids, you know that, don't you?"

"Thanks, I know," I mumble, struggling to keep from feeling guilty.

"Anything else you want to talk about, honey?"

"No, I'm alright."

"Okay." She fluffs up my hair, smiling sadly. "Now eat up your waffles. And bring the plate back into the kitchen."

"I will." I take a bite of waffle to make her feel better.

After she leaves, I put my fork down and sigh. It's 9:00, so Dad has already left for work. I wonder what Lorraine is doing in her room; if Eugene has contacted her about anything yet. I'm starting to wonder if I even *want* to use the Shoe if (or when) Briner gets back. I'm getting so sick of this whole business. I just want Mrs. Hazelton back so things can become normal again.

Agitated, I wander around my room, straightening things up compulsively. After a while, I decide I have nothing better to do than start on my summer reading list. Picking it up from my desk, I choose a book that I already have on my shelf. It's *Lord of the Flies*, by William Golding. I start on the first chapter, but my mind keeps drifting. After I discover that I'm reading the same sentence for the tenth time, I toss the book away. I force down a little bit more of my waffle, then bring the plate into the kitchen. Mom's in the living room and doesn't see me.

As I go back into the hallway, something suddenly rushes at me. I yelp, jumping up in the air. It's Lorraine; she has an excited look in her eye. Clamping my mouth shut with her hand, she whispers, "Eugene just called, Hunter. He said he has something important to tell us!"

"What?" If it's possible, my heart speeds up even faster.

"I don't know, he told me to get you—come on!" She grabs my hand, dragging me back through the hallway and into her room. The Glass is on her desk, shining up at the ceiling. I can see Eugene's head in it.

"Hello, Hunter, how's it going?" he says calmly as I come in. "I heard that the police were giving you some trouble."

"They are," I answer shakily. "They think we've got something to do with Esther Hazleton's disappearance."

"Well, you do in a way, don't you?" he answers. "You didn't tell them anything about the Teleporter, did you?"

"No."

"Or about the shop?"

"No."

"Good." He sighs. "We can't have the police hanging about here. Especially now that Artmas and Esther are back."

"What?!" My heart leaps up into my throat. "They're *back*?!"

"That they are." I can't see Eugene's features, but it sounds like he is grinning. "And they have the Teleporter with them. Why don't you come down and get it?"

Lorraine squeals and grabs me around my neck, nearly choking me in her glee. "Oh, let's go get it, Hunter! Let's not wait another minute!"

"But what about Mom?" I croak, trying to pry her hands off my neck.

"Who cares about Mom! We can sneak through a window again!"

I feel dazed and stunned. I can't believe that the Shoe is back in Abottsville. Or Mrs. Hazelton, either.

"But what if Mom sees—"

"She won't. Come on, let's go." She springs to the window and pries it open.

"Lorraine, stop!" I grab her arm. "We're going to get in trouble!"

"Oh, Hunter, don't wimp out on me now!" She yanks her arm away. "We've got to do this!"

Eugene, who has been listening to this whole conversation awkwardly, says, "Erm, maybe you better *not* do this, Lorraine. I mean, if it is only going to get you in trouble—"

Lorraine ignores him. To my horror, she scrambles out of the open window.

"Listen, I've got to talk to you later, Eugene," I gasp. Before he can say anything else, I grab the Glass and shove it in a drawer. Then I rush to the window and look out wildly. "*Lorraine,*" I whisper, panicking when I don't see her. Suddenly, a hand comes out of nowhere and grabs me by my polo shirt.

"What in the—"

Lorraine takes advantage of my surprise and drags me out of the window. I land in a heap at her feet.

"Lorraine, you idiot, you're going to get us killed!"

"Shut up," she hisses. "Briner's at the shop now with Mrs. Hazelton. We've got to get there."

I stagger to my feet just as a voice shouts, "Hey!" from the Hazelton's backyard. Both Lorraine and I wheel around.

It's Marty Hazelton.

He's standing stock still a few yards away, clutching a beer can in one hand, an overturned lawn chair behind him. "What in the hell are you kids doing?!"

Another completely unwelcome voice comes right after his. "Hunter? Lorraine? What are you doing out here? You're supposed to be grounded!"

Mom is staring out of Lorraine's window, a look of shock and anger on her face.

"Mom!" I shout wildly, no longer thinking straight. "I can explain!"

"Oh, he'll explain alright!" Mr. Hazelton roars. "Who's Briner? Where's my wife? Don't tell me you don't know! I just heard you talking about her! You're going to see her, aren't you?!"

I back up, knocking into Lorraine, suddenly not sure what to do. Then Lorraine grabs my collar, whispering into my ear, "*Run!*"

I take off like a shot, Lorraine hot on my heels. I hear Mom's cry of alarm and Marty's roar of rage but ignore both. Scrambling over our back fence, I land on my hands and knees in the alley. Lorraine lands beside me. As I jump upright, I throw a look over my shoulder. With a thrill of horror, I realize that Marty has decided to follow us. And he's following pretty closely.

"Come on, Hunter!" Lorraine shouts, already ahead of me. I put on a burst of speed and catch up to her, my heart pounding so hard I think it might burst out of my chest.

"Hazelton's f-f-following—"

"I know! We've just got to get there before he does!"

"Hey, you little brats, get back here!" I hear Mr. Hazelton scream from behind us.

Lorraine and I burst out of the alleyway and run full tilt down the street. People in their yards turn around to stare at us, then do a double take when they see Mr. Hazelton bearing down behind.

Lorraine cuts through somebody's lawn and I follow her, gasping. It's not too far to Monty's now, but will we make it?

As we turn onto Tuttle Street, a car has to slam on its brakes to avoid hitting us. Normally, a near collision would have given me a heart attack, but now I have bigger things on my mind. The driver sticks his head out the window, shouting "Hey, you kids—Mr. Hazelton?!"

I can't help it; I have to turn around. I need to know how close Mr. Hazelton is. But when I throw another look over my shoulder, I trip, my feet flying up from under me. I knock into Lorraine and send us both sprawling onto the sidewalk. Stars flash in front of my eyes.

Lorraine gets up before I do. I'm on my knees when I feel someone grab my collar and wrench me up. Mr. Hazelton! His face is red with rage and exertion. I try to shout out, but my voice get caught in my throat. My body goes limp, like a possum playing dead. Mr. Hazelton is shaking me back and forth. "You rotten, dirty little—"

"Hunter!"

Someone shouts my name. It's Lorraine. She had started running, but turns back when she realizes I have been caught. For some reason, the sight of her standing shocked and terrified a few yards away gives me sudden strength.

Mr. Hazelton is still shouting at me, despite the sight of several stunned bystanders.

"Oh yeah!" I finally shout back. "Well, take this, Mr. Hazelton!" I send my knee so hard into his groin that he gasps and loosens his grip. Wrenching away, I turn and flee. Monty's is straight up ahead. Nothing is going to stop us now.

CHAPTER SEVENTEEN

REUNION

Lorraine and I turn off the sidewalk and fly up the sagging steps of Briner's shop, bursting through the front door.

Briner, who's standing near his desk, jumps in surprise when we come barreling in. I guess he didn't expect us to get here so quickly.

"Mr. Thomas! Lorraine! What's—"

"Someone's chasing us!" Lorraine gasps, slamming the door shut behind her and locking it.

"Who?" Briner strides toward us. "Is it the police?"

"No, someone worse," I groan. "Marty Hazelton!"

"Marty Hazelton, who is that? Is that Esther Hazelton's husband?"

"Yeah, and he's coming to pick her up!"

Suddenly, there's a loud pounding on the door.

"It's him!" I whisper, terrified.

"Hey, you kids, I know you're in there! Bring my wife out!" Mr. Hazelton shouts.

When Briner hears this, he rounds on us, his eyes blazing. "You *told* him we had his wife here?!"

"Oh, no, of course not!" Lorraine exclaims.

"He sort of inferred it," I say meekly.

"Damn it," Briner curses, forking a hand through his hair. Mr. Hazelton is still pounding hard on the door. Suddenly, Briner darts away from us, rushing to a shelf along one wall. Snatching up a ball of string, he turns and runs back. Both Lorraine and I stare at the ball.

"Umm, Mr. Briner?" Lorraine says. "I don't really think a—"

"Silence," Briner snaps. "Open the door."

"What?!" I squawk. "Open the door? But I thought we didn't want him in here!"

"It's our only choice," he says grimly. "We can't leave him out there; he is attracting too much attention. Now," he gestures to Lorraine, "open the door."

Shaking slightly, she obeys his command. I watch in a daze as she unlocks the door and swings it wide open.

Marty bursts in the room like a bull on a rampage. And he's headed straight for me! I freeze in shock, thinking for the thousandth time in three days that I'm going to die. But before Mr. Hazelton can even reach me, Briner hurls the ball of string at him. The ball hits his chest and suddenly starts coming undone. Yards of string wrap around Mr. Hazelton's mouth, arms, and legs, moving like fast snakes intent on capture. In less than a minute, he is thoroughly trussed and lying helpless on the floor.

Still unable to believe what just happened, I look up at Briner. To my surprise, he grins at me. "Well, that didn't go as badly as you had thought, did it, Mr. Thomas?"

"No, I guess not," I answer, my voice coming out in a squeak.

"Oh, no," Lorraine says suddenly from the open doorway. I spin around quickly.

"What is it?"

She turns to me, her eyes wide. "The police are coming!"

"What?!" I rush to the door with Briner at my heels. We both stick our heads out. Sure enough, a patrol car is zooming down Tuttle Street. It brakes to a stop right in front of Monty's. My legs seem to give away for a second, and I clutch the doorjamb for support. *Could this situation get any worse?!*

"Somebody must have called the cops on Hazleton and us!" I gasp.

Briner, acting fast, slams the door shut. He whirls around. "Then we've got to get Hazelton out of here!" He rushes to where Mr. Hazelton is lying on the floor and yanks him up by the shoulders. "Come on, children, grab his legs!"

Lorraine and I don't ask any questions. We both grab a struggling Mr. Hazelton by his ankles and lift him off the floor. Carrying him, we all half-stumble, half-run to Briner's door behind his desk. Briner flings open the door with one hand and we shove Mr. Hazelton through. Just then, the cops start pounding to be let in.

"Police, open up!"

"Oh no, oh no..." I moan.

"Don't freak out now, Hunter," Lorraine gasps, slamming the door behind us.

"Let's go," Briner orders. We all start jogging laboriously down the stone passageway. Mr. Hazelton is being jostled up and down between us, but that doesn't stop him from struggling. His shoes keep twisting back and forth against my wrists.

"Gosh, he's heavy," I pant.

"Just keep a hold on him," Briner answers, panting himself.

It seems to take forever for us to finally reach Briner's rooms. He opens the door and we carry Mr. Hazelton inside. I glance nervously around, but the chairs and desks cluttered in the room don't move. *They probably won't attack while Briner's here*, I reassure myself.

"Do you want to leave him here, Mr. Briner?" Lorraine asks, pushing some hair out of her sweaty face. But before Briner can answer, a door along the wall opens and Eugene walks in.

"Eugene!" Lorraine and I both exclaim.

"Hey, what's going on?!" He looks in surprise at the bound Mr. Hazelton.

"I'll tell you in a moment, Eugene," Briner pants. Then he adds, "We'll bring him into the bedroom, children."

The first thing I notice when we get inside the room is a bed. A bed on which *Mrs. Hazelton* is sitting. At the sight of us, she springs up.

"Marty?!"

At the sound of his wife's voice, Mr. Hazelton begins squirming even harder. We heave him onto the bed, and his wife rushes to him.

"Oh, Marty, what have they done to you?"

"Nothing serious," Briner mutters.

"But what's going on?" Eugene says. "Who is this?"

"My husband," Mrs. Hazelton snaps at him.

Since Eugene still looks mystified, Briner explains, "Mr. Hazelton followed the children here when he discovered that we had his wife in the shop. I had to constrain him, naturally."

"Damn it," Eugene shakes his head. "This is going to complicate things."

Suddenly, there's a muffled commotion from upstairs in the shop. It sounds like the cops have just broken in.

"Oh yes, I forgot to mention," Briner says grimly. "The police are here, too."

"The police?!" Eugene and Mrs. Hazelton exclaim together.

"I assume someone contacted them when they saw all the commotion around here," Briner says. He moves to a chair and sinks down on it, looking suddenly weary.

"Well, at least the children are here," Eugene says. He turns to us, pulling something out of his pocket. A cracked, brown, moldy something. The Shoe.

For a moment, Lorraine and I can only stare at it. It looks exactly the same as it did three days ago, when we first set eyes on it in Monty's shop. It's hard to believe that such a small, insignificant-looking object has caused such big problems for all of us. I feel dizzy just thinking about it.

"Go on." Eugene grins. "It's yours now."

Slowly, almost cautiously, Lorraine steps forward and takes the Shoe from Eugene's hand. "Thank you," she breathes. "Oh, thank you, Eugene!"

"Don't thank me," Eugene replies, still grinning. "Thank Arty. He was the one who traveled all the way to California to get it for you!"

"Oh, of course!" she cries. She darts to where Briner is sitting and throws her arms around his neck. "Thank you, Mr. Briner! I owe you so much!"

Briner looks startled, and even more startled when Lorraine kisses him on the cheek.

"That wasn't really necessary," he mutters, rubbing his cheek as Lorraine steps away. "But you're welcome, Miss Thomas."

I glance over at Mrs. Hazelton sitting on the bed next to her husband. Her face looks grim. *I bet she wishes she was still in California right now*, I think to myself.

"Now that they have the Shoe, can you let my husband go?" she asks Briner coldly.

"Not just yet, Madam," Briner replies, standing up. "There is something I must do before I let you leave." And he pulls a brown paper bag out of his suit pocket.

I gasp. "The Amnesia Dust!"

"Exactly right." Briner gestures to Eugene, who steps forward reluctantly and grabs hold of Mrs. Hazelton.

"Wait, what's going on?" she cries. "What are you doing?"

"Standard procedure, Madam," Briner answers calmly, but his eyes are glittering. Beside them, Mr. Hazelton begins to buck and squirm on the bed. Watching this, I feel sick.

"What are you doing this for? Can't you just let them go?" I squeak out.

"Don't be stupid, boy," Briner snaps at me. "We can't release these people until they're properly Dusted. They know too much about the shop. They could ruin us!"

"It's for our own security, Hunter," Eugene tells me, almost pleading. "Please understand."

I don't know how to answer. Mrs. Hazelton is beginning to struggle. "I—why would we want to ruin your shop?" she pants. "Just let us go!"

Briner snorts, hatred in his eyes. "And the instant we do so, you and your husband would scamper straight upstairs to the police and tell them about the big, bad men who had you trapped down here. And frankly, we can't risk that."

"Then what *are* you going to do with us?"

"Dust you and send you out the back door. Then you can go back to your home, and you'll not remember that any of this happened," he replies airily.

"I think I see a flaw in your plan, Mr. Briner," I speak up. "Aren't the neighbors and the police going to wonder why Mr. and Mrs. Hazelton can't remember anything about what happened to them?"

"Is it my problem if everyone thinks the Hazeltons are going senile?" Briner snaps his fingers. "Now let's get this over with, Eugene."

Eugene nods grimly, looking as if he doesn't want this to happen any more than I do. I close my eyes and hold my breath, turning away. I feel a hand touch mine; Lorraine's. I grip her fingers tightly.

Suddenly, there's a sound of wood splintering and breaking open upstairs. My eyes jerk open as we all whirl around.

"Damn it," Briner hisses. "The police must have broken through the door behind my desk. They'll be here any moment."

"I'll go reset the wards," Eugene says quickly. He releases Mrs. Hazelton and rushes out the bedroom door as if he has only been looking for an excuse to get out of the room. To our surprise, Mrs. Hazelton rushes after him.

"We're here, we're in here!" she cries, obviously trying to alert the police. But she doesn't get very far. Briner grabs her and twists her around.

"Shut up, do you hear me, shut up!" he hisses. "One more word out of your mouth and you'll be on the bed next to your husband!" He shoves her away. She wisely shuts her mouth, her eyes wide and frightened. I know exactly how Mrs. Hazelton feels at the moment, and it's not very good.

Briner turns away. He starts pacing back and forth, muttering under his breath. He seems to be thinking very hard, and I watch him warily.

Suddenly, Briner looks back toward Lorraine and me. For some odd reason, he's staring at the Shoe clutched in Lorraine's hand.

"Lorraine, Mr. Thomas," he says slowly, "could I see you alone for a moment?"

I gulp. *This isn't going to be good.*

"Oh, of course," Lorraine says.

"Good. Then follow me." He gestures to us and we follow him out of the room. My heart's pounding again. I don't like the thought of going anywhere with Briner, but there's nothing I can do about it now. Briner leads us down a narrow stone hallway and opens the first door on the right. I hang back behind Lorraine, but she whispers, "Oh, relax, Hunter. It's only a bathroom."

I peek over Lorraine's shoulder. Sure enough, it's only a bathroom. And a rather clean one, at that.

"Sit down, please," Briner says, holding the door open for us. We both go in; Lorraine sits on the edge of the tub, so I am forced to take the toilet seat.

Briner shuts the door and faces us. "Children, I'd like to tell you a story."

"Ooh, a story," Lorraine says.

Briner clasps his hands in front of him. "It starts in my own homeland," he says. "Igarthia."

"Igarthia?" I ask. "Where's that?" Suddenly I realize something. "It isn't that funny island I saw on the Teleportation Tracker, is it?"

"It is indeed," Briner answers. "My brother and I were born and raised there. When we were older, we went into business together. A shop called Monty's, named after my dead father."

"Oh, I'm so sorry," Lorraine says sympathetically.

Briner waves his hand. "That was a long time ago, Lorraine."

He pauses for a moment, then continues. "You should know our shop was shut down a few months ago, for...er...selling faulty products. Eugene and I couldn't do business in Igarthia anymore. So we moved here. To the States. We hoped that business here would be better. But it has not.

"What I mean to say is—well, look at this disaster!" He sighs heavily, shaking his head. "One small Teleporter has created such a problem that I don't think our shop will be able to survive it. I am beginning to think I have no other choice but this..."

Briner turns to stare at us. The look in his eyes makes me shrink back on my toilet seat.

"I must have that Teleporter back," Briner states quietly.

CHAPTER EIGHTEEN

THE ULTIMATUM

"What?" Lorraine cries. "The Shoe? But why, Mr. Briner?"

"Because I must leave this place as soon as possible to return to Igarthia, Lorraine," he replies impatiently. "And *that* Teleporter you are holding in your hand is the only way."

"But what about us?" I squeak.

"What about you?" he snaps.

"Well, what are we going to do after you leave with the Shoe?"

"*You*," he says with emphasis, "are going to stay here in the shop and Dust the Hazeltons and the police when they come through the door. We can't have them remembering anything.

"Now," he holds his hand out to Lorraine. "The Shoe."

183

Lorraine clutches the Shoe to her chest, her eyes wide. She looks as if she can't believe what's happening. I can't believe it either. I feel dizzy, like I'm about to fall off the toilet seat any moment.

"The Shoe," Briner repeats.

"But, but what if I don't want to give it back?" Lorraine gasps.

"That is not an option," Briner answers. "I *need* it."

Lorraine stands up and turns to me, desperation in her eyes. My heart is pounding wildly, but I think I have an idea. The only question is, will I be able to pull it off?

Suddenly, there's a commotion outside our little bathroom. It sounds like the police have found the door that leads to Briner's rooms and are trying to break in. Momentarily distracted, Briner looks away from us. This is it, my only chance!

Leaping at Lorraine, I shout, "Come on, let's Teleport!" If we could just get out of here—

But before Lorraine can even open her mouth, Briner whirls back around in surprise.

"You weak, sniveling little fool!" he shouts, grabbing me and shoving me away from Lorraine. "Don't even *think* of doing that! Do you hear me?!"

"Y-yes, Mr. Briner," I squeak. *So much for good plans.*

184

Lorraine seems to be thinking the same thing, because she glares at me as I sink back on the toilet seat. "Could you have been any faster, Speedy Gonzalez?"

"Shut up," I mutter at her. "I didn't hear *you* come up with any ideas."

"Neither of you are 'coming up' with anything," Briner snaps. He pulls the bag of Amnesia Dust out of his pocket and holds it up in the air. "Now, I don't want to do this, but I will if I have to."

"But Mr. Briner..." Lorraine whines.

"No buts," Briner says firmly. "I need that Shoe."

Lorraine stares up at him tremulously. Staring back at her, the cold anger in Briner's face almost seems to soften slightly for a moment.

Before I can really comprehend what I'm seeing, Briner clears his throat and says, "Lorraine, you know I have no choice."

Lorraine is quiet for a long time. Both Briner and I stare at her, wondering what she's going to do next. Then she says shakily, her head bowed, "Alright. But Mr. Briner, can Hunter and I have a moment alone...to say goodbye to the Shoe?"

Briner's eyebrows jerk down suspiciously. "To say goodbye to the Shoe? Alone?"

"Yes."

"I'm afraid that's not possible."

"But, Mr. Briner!" She looks up at him hurtfully. "I thought you trusted us!"

Briner snorts. "When did I ever say I trusted you?" But when Lorraine continues to look at him with a hurt face, he rolls his eyes and says, "Oh, alright! You may have *one* minute alone with the Shoe. One minute. But if you try to escape with it, be warned—I have the Teleportation Tracker and when I find you, the punishments...the punishments *will* be severe." Then he gives us one last glare before spinning on his heel and leaving the bathroom.

"Well, that was scary," I say. Suddenly, Lorraine sits back down on the tub and bursts into tears.

Startled, I drop down beside her. "Lorraine, what's wrong?"

"I can't—I can't believe I'm going to give up the Shoe," she blubbers.

"But we *have* to, remember?" I say, nearly feeling as bad as she does.

"I know," she sniffs, "but we never got to use it and now we never will!"

I'm not sure what else to do but pat her hand consolingly. For awhile, we just sit together and reflect on all of this. Finally, Lorraine takes a shaky breath and says, "Well, it's for the best, isn't it? We're doing the right thing. Mr. Briner needs the Shoe more than we do." She's looking at me earnestly. For some reason, I feel a lump in my throat. I swallow it down and nod.

"Well," she sighs, "g-goodbye then, my Shoe." She bends her head and gives the smelly Teleporter a slobbery kiss. I wrinkle my nose at this but decide not to say anything. Just then, a knock on the door interrupts our emotional moment.

"Who is it?" I call reluctantly.

"It is I," Briner's voice answers. "Your minute is up. I'm coming in."

The door opens. Briner enters, followed by Eugene, whose guilty expression tells me he's already learned about Briner's new escape plan.

"So," Briner stands before us. "May I have the Teleporter now?"

I look at Lorraine and she looks at me. We both nod to each other. Then Lorraine gets to her feet and very slowly, very nobly (nearly like the Queen of England herself) walks up to Briner and sets the Shoe in his hand. "Your Teleporter, Mr. Briner."

"Thank you, Lorraine," Briner says with a barely perceptible sigh of relief. He starts to pull the Shoe away, but for some reason, she still has a grip on it. "I *knew—*" (Briner gives the Shoe a particularly hard yank and manages to free it) "—you would do the right thing. Thank you."

Lorraine sniffs.

"So are you leaving now?" I ask. I'm already trying to forget what Lorraine and I have just given away.

"No, not yet," he says. "Remember, I had a job for you, Mr. Thomas."

"What was that?" I ask uneasily.

"To Dust both the police and the Hazeltons," he answers. "I have conveniently tied the Hazeltons up in the bedroom for you, so that won't be a problem."

"What about the cops?"

"They should not be a problem, *either*," he replies. "Merely sprinkle some Dust on them as soon as they come through the door."

"Um, okay." I nod, but I think Briner's making this duty sound a lot easier than it's going to be. Ignoring the tight feeling in my stomach, I take the bag of Amnesia Dust from him.

"Good." He turns to Eugene. "So ready to go?"

"Er, not yet," Eugene answers, looking guiltily over at Lorraine and me. "Are you children alright with this?"

"Umm..."

"Sure..."

Not that we can really do anything about it now, I think to myself bitterly.

Eugene's guilty expression remains. "I know this must be so disappointing...to see the Shoe taken from you again...but, here—I have something to give you."

He digs into his pocket and pulls out a small, round, gray puffball, about the size of my palm.

I stare at it. "What is it?"

"It's a Weather Puff," he replies proudly. "My first ever invention! It tells you the weather—red for hot, blue for cold, and green for in-between."

"But now it's gray," Lorraine points out.

"Oh, that's because we're inside," Eugene explains. "It only works outdoors. Here." And he hands the puffball to me.

"Uh, thanks, I guess," I say, putting it in my pocket.

"Now you'll always have a little piece of magic in your pocket, wherever you go!" Eugene declares. Behind him, I think I see Briner roll his eyes.

Suddenly, there's a sound of splintering wood and shouting voices. I jump, clutching the bag of Amnesia Dust to my chest. It sounds like the police have finally broken in! I'd almost forgotten about them.

"The police," Briner mutters. "*Now* are you ready to go, Eugene?"

"Wait!" Lorraine cries, leaping forward. Grabbing Briner's arm, she looks into both brother's faces. "Will Hunter and I ever see you again?"

Briner looks uncertain of what to say. But Eugene answers reassuringly, "Of course you will! Listen, I will send you a memo as soon as we get back in Igarthia."

Now, there's a loud pounding on the bathroom door.

"Police! Open up!" bawls the now familiar voice of Officer Jim Meyers.

"Come on, Eugene!" Briner says, thrusting the Shoe towards him impatiently. "Let's go!"

"Wait!" Lorraine cries. "You haven't got my address, Eugene!"

"Don't worry!" Eugene says back as he puts his hand on the Shoe Briner's holding out for him. "Memos work by magic!"

And those are his last words to us as Briner shouts, "Take us to Igarthia!"

For a split-second, nothing happens. All of us seem to be suspended in our places—me, standing stock-still next to the toilet seat with Lorraine; Briner and Eugene standing in the center of the room together, clutching the Shoe. Then a sudden gust of wind makes me stumble backward against the tub. Squinting, I see Briner and Eugene spinning around and around together until they both become a blur. The wind becomes so strong and fast that I'm flung backward, landing hard on the bottom of the

tub. Forcing myself up on my elbows, I can see Lorraine crouched on the floor near me, covering her head with her hands as the wind swirls around us.

"Lorraine, quick, get in the tub!" I shout, conveniently remembering my tornado safety tips from school. She manages to push herself up and I help her crawl into the tub beside me. Together, we cower down behind the shelter of the porcelain wall as the whirlwind created by the

Teleporter rages around us. And then, just when I think I can't stand it anymore, it stops. For a moment, we are too stunned to move. Then, slowly, we raise our heads and peer over the edge of the tub. The place where Briner and Eugene were standing only a moment ago is now empty.

They've Teleported.

"Police! Open up!" a voice shouts suddenly, making us both jump. "I know you're in there! Don't make me break this door down!"

"Oh, the cops!" Lorraine gasps, temporarily forgetting her accent. "Do you still have your bag, Hunter?"

I look down at my right hand, where I had been holding the bag only moments before. But now, to my horror, I realize my hand is empty.

"Th-the bag's gone!"

"No, it can't be! What did you do with it?!"

"I don't know!" I start to look around frantically, feeling sick. *How could I lose the bag at a critical time like this*?! "It must have blown out of my hand with the wind!"

"Well, find it, quick!"

There's a pounding on the door again. "Open up!" Meyers shouts. "This is the last time we're asking nicely!"

"Oh, there it is!" Lorraine cries, pointing. "Behind the toilet seat!"

I lunge forward, snatching up the bag. By some miracle, it's still closed and none of the Dust has gotten out. I'm so relieved I feel weak.

"Thank you, thank you, thank you!" I say out loud to God.

"Don't thank *me*," Lorraine snips. "Wait until you've Dusted the cops!"

I turn towards her pleadingly. "Can't *you* do it?"

"No! Remember what Briner said? He wanted you to do it!"

I start to object, but then Meyers calls, "Alright, kids, I've given you long enough. I'm breakin' this door down."

"Oh, no," I moan, feeling weak, but now from fear. "I can't do this!"

"Okay, kids, stand back!" Meyers yells.

"Of course you can, Hunter, I know you can!" Lorraine shouts over his voice.

"I can't—"

BAM.

Chapter nineteen

When the Dust Settles

The bathroom door flies open and slams against the wall. Two officers, Jim Meyers and Ryan Wilson, burst into the room with their guns drawn. It all happens so suddenly I can only feel shock. Then Lorraine grabs my shoulders and shouts, "Do it now, Hunter!"

At that moment, Wilson lunges towards me. I feel my hand, as if it's acting by itself, plunge into the bag and grab a handful of dust. When Wilson's fingers are only inches away from my shirt collar, I hurl the handful of glittery gold dust into both officers' faces. They act like they've been hit with pepper spray, staggering backward and sneezing helplessly. I can only watch, frozen in place, as they try to swipe the dust off their faces. Then Wilson looks up, squinting, an expression of dazed confusion on his face.

"Hey," he says, "where *am* I?"

I let out my breath in a whoosh as I feel my heart start beating again. Lorraine throws her arms around me.

"Oh, Hunter, it worked, it worked! I knew you could do it!"

"I *did* do it," I breathe. I can't completely believe it myself. Meanwhile, Wilson and Meyers start to wander around the bathroom with bemused expressions on their faces.

"So, where are we, Chief?" Wilson asks, scratching his head. "I can't figure it out."

"Hey." Meyers points suddenly at Lorraine and me. "They might know. Do you know?"

Lorraine and I exchange uncertain glances.

"Um," I say. "Well, you're in...ah..."

"Oh, we don't know where you are," Lorraine butts in quickly, nodding her head. "Yes, we don't know."

"Dangit," Meyers says. "I thought you might know."

Wilson is standing near the sink, turning the tap on and off in wonderment. "Hey, Chief. Come over and look at this!"

When Meyers wanders over to check it out, I shake my head. It looks like the Dust is powerful even in small amounts. Then, turning towards Lorraine, I ask, "So what do we do now?"

"Well, we still have to Dust the Hazelton's, don't we?" she answers. "I suppose we don't have any choice except to leave them here and go.

"Excuse me, Officers," she clears her throat. "Hunter and I have to go now. To, um...find out where you are. So you just stay here. Don't leave."

"We won't," Wilson answers cheerfully, giving her a salute before returning to the sink. We exit the bathroom together and start down the hallway. As I tiptoe behind Lorraine, I think firmly to myself, *Briner tied the Hazeltons up, so they should be easy to Dust. You can do this, Hunter.* But I don't quite believe myself as Lorraine and I both peer around the corner into Briner's bedroom. Mrs. Hazelton is tied up to a chair. There's a look of fear and exhaustion on her face; obviously, she's been struggling against her bonds for awhile. Mr. Hazelton is still lying in the same position on the bed, covered up in string.

"Come on," Lorraine whispers, giving me a little push. "Let's go."

Swallowing, I force my shaking legs to move forward into the room behind Lorraine. When Mrs. Hazelton catches sight of us, a look of relief crosses her face.

"Hunter and Lorraine! Thank God you're alright! What's going on?"

I stop and stare at her. "Uh..." I say. Suddenly, I'm not sure what to do. The look of clear relief on Mrs. Hazelton's face has frozen me. *This is my neighbor*, I think to myself. *Yes, she stole the Shoe from us, but is that any reason to inflict the Dust on her?*

Lorraine prods me in the shoulder. "Go on, Hunter," she whispers. "What are you waiting for?"

I shake my head. "No, I'm—I'm not going to do it."

Both Mrs. Hazelton and Lorraine stare at me in confusion.

"Do what?" Mrs. Hazelton asks, but before I can answer her, Lorraine says quickly, "Can you excuse us for a moment, Mrs. Hazelton?"

"Um, I suppose so…"

"Good." Lorraine pulls me out of the room and back into the hallway.

"What do you mean you're not going to do it, Hunter?" she whispers fiercely as soon as we're out of earshot.

"They don't need to be Dusted, okay?" I hiss back.

"But we have to! Briner said—"

"Never mind what Briner said," I interrupt her. "The only reason he wanted us to Dust the Hazeltons is so they couldn't go blabbing about Monty's and the Teleporter. But do you think they're really going to tell anybody about this stuff? Not unless they want them to think they're crazy!"

Lorraine stares at me. "So you trust them, then?"

"Yes!"

"Even *Mr.* Hazelton?"

I pause. I'd almost forgotten about Marty. *But you can't Dust one and not the other, can you?* I think to myself. "Yes, I trust him, too," I force myself to answer.

Lorraine takes a deep breath, then tiptoes to the end of hallway and peers around the corner. Then she tiptoes back to me.

"Alright," she says in a resigned voice. "We won't Dust them. But we have to make them promise not to tell—"

"We will," I say grimly. "Let's go back in."

Together, we walk into the bedroom. As soon as Mrs. Hazelton sees us, she says anxiously, "But kids, what's going on?"

"Um, we can untie you first, if you want, Mrs. Hazelton," I say. I'm not even sure *how* to explain what's going on just yet.

"Oh, yes, please untie me," Mrs. Hazelton says, "These nasty ropes..."

As I go around to her, she adds, "And please untie Marty, too."

I gulp, but there's nothing I can do about it now as Lorraine goes around to the bed. I force my attention back to the ropes around Mrs. Hazelton's hands and feet.

"Thank you, Hunter," she says as soon as I untie her, rubbing her wrists and standing up.

"You're welcome," I say, then turn around to check Lorraine's progress on Mr. Hazelton. She's working on the very last knot.

197

"There!" she declares when she's finally done. "You can get up now, Mr.—"

But to our surprise, the string suddenly starts unraveling by itself. Mrs. Hazelton gasps and steps backward. As the string keeps unraveling past Mr. Hazelton's waist and legs, he manages to sit up, an expression of shock on his face. Then, with a *whishing* noise, all of it falls off his body and starts winding together again. Before we know it, a compact and completely innocent-looking ball of string is lying on the bed.

"Wow!" Lorraine exclaims beside me.

Mr. Hazelton turns toward his wife, stunned. "Esther..."

To our surprise, Mrs. Hazelton rushes forward and throws her arms around him. "Oh, Marty, you're okay! I've missed you so much!"

"I've missed you, too, Esther!" he exclaims. "What *is* this place?"

"I'm not sure," Mrs. Hazelton answers, "I think it's some kind of shop, but I've never been in here before, either."

A look of confusion crosses Mr. Hazelton's face. "But isn't this the place where they were keeping you hostage?" he demands.

Mrs. Hazelton looks equally confused. "Keeping me hostage?"

"Yes!" he says impatiently. "Esther, don't you know you've been missing for three days?!"

"Of course I know, Marty!" Mrs. Hazelton's face flushes. "But you see, I—I left. On my own."

Marty stares at her. "On your own? You *left*? You weren't... kidnapped?"

"No."

"But—how?"

Mrs. Hazelton wrings her hands. She looks unable to answer in the face of her husband's disbelief. Turning towards Lorraine and me, she asks uneasily, "Um, children? Maybe you can help me explain?"

"Oh, I can do it!" Lorraine exclaims eagerly. She turns to Marty and clasps her hands in front of her like a British schoolmistress. "You see, Mr. Hazelton, it all started four days ago, when Hunter and I were walking home from school..."

About an hour of her monologue later, my sister declares, "So do you see now, Mr. Hazelton? It was all the result of one little shoe."

Mr. Hazelton is still sitting on the bed, his arms folded across his chest. "I see..." he says slowly. He looks stunned by the story. Then he says in a dazed voice, "Good thing Esther's back, though."

"Oh, Marty," Esther cries, startling us. She throws her arms around him again. "I knew you would say that! I know how much you care now!"

"But you always knew!" Mr. Hazelton splutters, still looking a little dazed.

"No, I didn't always know!" She pulls away from him and stares tearfully into his face. "Don't you see? That's why I left, because I *didn't* know you still cared about me. I wanted to get away for a bit, have time to think on my own. When I found out about the Shoe, it felt like destiny. I knew—" she glances at Lorraine and me with an apologetic look, "—I knew I had to take it. I'm sorry, children. I only intended to be gone until that night! But once I started traveling, I wanted to keep going."

She grips Marty's arm, sniffs, and continues. "I *always* was going to come back, Marty. That's why I never contacted you. I just ended up staying away longer than I expected. When that terrible man showed up, I realized I *wanted* to go home! I missed you so much, Marty. And I felt guilty for never telling you where I was."

"You should have told me." Mr. Hazelton's voice is strained. "I was worried sick!"

Mrs. Hazelton looks down. "I know, but I couldn't bear to contact you. I was so confused....but now I realize. I realize how much you care about me, my—my Snuggy Wumpcake!"

"'My Snuggy Wumpcake!'" Mr. Hazelton cries. "You haven't called me that in ten years!"

200

When they start to exchange passionate kisses, I look away in embarrassment. Lorraine is still watching them raptly, so I pinch her arm.

"I think it's time to go now," I whisper, red-faced.

Lorraine turns around to glare at me, but when she sees my face, she rolls her eyes. "Oh, *alright*," she whispers, letting me lead her out of the room. As soon as we get out into the hallway though, she swoons, saying, "That was such a romantic moment!"

"Yeah...romantic." I suppress a shudder. "They probably need a few moments now. Let's go check on the cops."

When we get to the bathroom door, we go in carefully, looking around. Wilson is reading one of the magazines near the toilet and Meyers is sitting on the edge of the tub, playing with his badge.

"Oh, there you are," Wilson says in relief when he sees us. "We were getting bored. Have you found out where we are yet?"

"Oh, yes, we have," Lorraine answers. "You're in...an old abandoned shop."

"A shop!" Wilson shakes his head. "I can't think how we got in here. Last thing I remember, we were at the station."

"Oh, the police station!" Lorraine says, as if she's suddenly realized something. "You're probably needed there now."

"You bet we are!" Wilson exclaims, looking at his watch. "It's almost break-time. Doug said he was bringing jelly donuts today."

"There's gonna be some confusion around the police station when Wilson and Meyers show up not remembering anything," I mutter, guiltily shoving the bag of Amnesia Dust deeper in my pocket.

"Don't worry," Lorraine replies haughtily. "I have a way of solving that." Then she turns back to the cops and says in a loud, clear voice, "Excuse me, gentlemen. When both of you get back to the police station, tell the other officers that when you came here, you found Esther Hazelton and took her back home, so everything's okay."

Wilson frowns. "But why would we want to do that?"

"Oh, because it will get you more jelly donuts."

Wilson grins. "Okay, then. We'll do it."

I turn towards Lorraine in surprise. "How did you know to do that?!"

She smirks. "Haven't you ever read about hypnotists before?"

I roll my eyes, but don't reply. *Dumb Lorraine.*

Then Meyers, who is still sitting on the tub, asks, "So can we go now?"

"I suppose so," Lorraine answers. "The Hazeltons should be ready by now."

We all leave the bathroom together and go down the hallway. When we get to the end, Lorraine calls from behind the corner, "Oh, may we come in, Mrs. Hazelton?"

"Yes, you can come in," I hear Mrs. Hazelton answer.

We all file inside. The Hazeltons are sitting on the bed together, their arms around each other's shoulders. Mrs. Hazelton's face is still tearstained, but she looks happier.

"I'm alright now, children." She smiles at us.

"That's good," Lorraine says. "We, ah, were thinking of leaving the shop now, Mr. and Mrs. Hazelton. Are you both ready?"

"Oh yes, we are," Mrs. Hazelton answers. "Are *they* alright, though?" She looks a little concernedly at the police behind us.

"Oh, they're fine." Lorraine turns to look at them. "Amnesia Dust doesn't have any lasting effects."

"Amnesia what?" Wilson asks.

"Oh, never mind that," Lorraine says quickly, her face reddening. "We should all be going now."

So our motley little group troops out of Briner's rooms. We start down the stone corridor that leads upstairs to the infamous shop. We're all silent as we walk along, each deep in our own thoughts. I put my hand in my pocket and touch Eugene's little Weather Puff, looking up at the fire-lighted torches bracketed on the walls. It all seems so unreal, but what's even *more* unreal is that I'll never see this place again. I feel a numb relief, and only the briefest smidge of sadness.

When we finally get upstairs to the shop, Lorraine turns to the Hazelton's. "You can go now, if you'd like. Hunter—" she looks at me, "and I are going to stay here a little while longer."

"Are you sure, dear?" Mrs. Hazelton asks in a concerned way.

"Yes, I'm sure," Lorraine replies firmly.

A look of sudden understanding crosses Mrs. Hazelton's face. "Alright, then," she says. "I suppose we should go now."

"Goodbye, Mr. and Mrs. Hazelton," I say.

"Goodbye, Hunter," Mrs. Hazelton replies, then nudges her husband, who has been gazing around the little shop.

"Oh, yeah," he grunts, looking around. "Goodbye, uh, Hunter."

"Goodbye, sir," I say, feeling a slight relief. It's hard to tell, but I think we've reconciled. He's not glaring at me, anyway.

He nods stiffly, then Wilson butts in, saying, "So can we go now, too?"

"Oh, of course," Lorraine replies. "There's a back door right there."

I watch as the cops and the Hazeltons go to the door and open it. Wilson, Meyers, and Marty walk out without looking back. But Mrs. Hazelton, who is holding her husband's hand, turns around and gives us a quick wave. I wave back as the door shuts behind them. *It looks like all of them are going to be alright*, I think to myself. Taking a deep breath, I turn towards Lorraine. She's gazing at the shelves along the opposite wall, where once, a million days ago, I picked up the smelly old shoe that would change my life forever.

"Amazing, isn't it?" she whispers.

"Yes," I say truthfully. "It *is* amazing."

She smiles sadly. "I can't believe it's over, though."

"Don't worry, Lorraine." I take her hand and give it a squeeze. "Maybe we'll have other adventures some day." I personally feel that another adventure isn't necessary at this moment, but I want to cheer her up. Then I say, "I think what happened was meant to be."

Lorraine turns toward me, then laughs suddenly. "Oh, Hunter, you're a philosopher now!"

"Really?" I say, brightening up. I'd never been called a philosopher before. "Does that mean I'm not still a wimp?"

She rolls her eyes. "No, you're still a little bit of a wimp. But maybe that's a good thing. It got us through this adventure, didn't it?"

"You're right, it did!" I exclaim, looking around the little shop with a sudden feeling of pride. After a moment I say, "So are you ready to go now?"

Lorraine takes a final sigh, then squares her shoulders. "Oh, yes, I'm ready. Let's go."

I start towards the back door, but she tugs on my hand. "No. Let's go through the front."

So together we go to the front door and swing it open, marching down the stairs. A lone bystander gazes at us with his mouth slightly open. We breeze past him and start to go down the sidewalk. Before we get barely three steps, I feel a very odd sensation, like some otherworldly wind has just passed over me. The hairs on the back of my neck prickle up, and I turn instinctively back to Monty's.

But the shop is gone.

It takes a moment for my mind to register what I'm seeing. The shop *is* gone. Now, there's only a mere alleyway between the A&P Grocery store and Half-Price Books.

"*Lorraine*," I hiss, tugging on her hand.

Lorraine turns around. I hear a gasp catch in her throat. She sees it, too. Or, more technically, she *doesn't* see it. After a moment, we look back towards each other, but don't speak. Somehow, we both know this isn't a time for words. Finally, hand in hand, we turn and start back home.

EPILOGUE

Exactly a week later, on a fresh Monday morning, I wake up. Stretching and yawning, I pull out of my pink elephant pajamas and into a pair of jeans and a shirt. After walking into the kitchen, I meet Mom, who still looks a little dazed. This is mostly due to the aftereffect of the Amnesia Dust Lorraine and I had given her. We had managed to give some to Dad, too. Conveniently, they had both forgotten about everything the next moment, including our groundings.

"Hi, sweetie," Mom says vaguely to me over the oven.

"Hi, Mom," I say, feeling only a momentary, trifling guilt. "I'm going out for awhile."

"Okay, sweetie, have fun."

Out on the street, I walk along leisurely. I'm heading down to Mabee's Ice Cream Parlor for a little breakfast. Suddenly, I hear a puffing noise behind me and look around. It's Officer Jim Meyers, who's moving slowly on a bicycle and sweating profusely.

"Hi, Officer Meyers," I say without thinking.

He looks up, startled. "Oh hey, uhh...Harry."

"Actually, it's Hunter," I say, somewhat embarrassed.

"Oh, right, Hunter." Meyers grins, pulling up beside me. "Actually, you should be glad I don't remember your name, sonny. Unlike some of the boys I got down at the station..."

"Right." I laugh nervously.

With a friendly wave goodbye, Meyers pedals on by me, still puffing. Feeling relieved, I continue on to the ice cream parlor.

After getting a double scoop of sherbet, I skip over to Tuttle Street. Licking my sherbet and walking slowly, I stare at the place where Monty's used to be. There's only that narrow alleyway between the Half-Price Bookstore and the A&P Grocery store. It's like the shop was never there.

Over the past week, I had been listening to other people in town, curious if any of them were going to mention the missing shop. No one did. Briner's wards must have done their job...only a few people, like me and Lorraine, had been able to see the shop. Sighing deeply, I turn to head home.

Back at the house, I'm waylaid by Lorraine in the hallway.

"Hunter, Hunter, I got an answer!" she squeals.

"From who, Eugene?" I ask, my heart skipping a beat.

She nods excitedly and I follow her into her room. On her desk are two small slips of white paper. The first is a memo that Eugene had sent us a few days ago. It reads, in neat, slanted handwriting—

Hunter and Lorraine,

Artmas and I have just arrived in Igarthia and set up shop in a new part of town. We're making some improvements and I think it will work this time. How are you two doing?

Eugene

Lorraine had been thrilled to receive the memo; even I'd been a little glad to hear back from Eugene. We had sent our reply on Sunday, saying how we were fine and wishing him and Briner good luck on the new shop. Now Lorraine picks up the new memo. We bend our heads together to read—

Hunter and Lorraine,

Glad to hear you're doing fine! Business here is moving slowly but surely. Of course, I'd love for you to see the shop in person one day. I'll try to send you some more photos next memo.

Eugene

"*More* photos!" I say. "Does that mean..."

"Yes!" Lorraine answers, grinning. "Eugene sent us a photograph!"

She picks up a black and white photo from her desk, showing it to me. There's Eugene smiling at us through his mustache, wearing a top hat. A.T. Briner is standing beside him, dressed somberly in a black suit and frowning. Behind them is what looks like the front of a shop. A sign in bold letters reads "Monty's." The shop looks like it's set on an old-fashioned cobblestone street. I flip the photo over. On the back, Eugene has written today's date, June 6th, 2008, and underneath it, "*Our new shop in Igarthia.*"

"Igarthia," I mutter under my breath. It's still pretty unbelievable.

"Oh yes, Igarthia," Lorraine says. "How I wish I was there! Do you think he would ever invite us? He wrote he would love for us to see the shop in person!"

I'm skeptical. "I bet we're not allowed to go over there, though. You know, us non-wizards." I myself don't

210

have any real desire to see Igarthia. The Shoe adventure was enough to last me a lifetime.

"Oh, I know." Lorraine sighs and wanders over to the bed. "But maybe one day we could...."

"Maybe," I concede. "So, do you still regret what happened? I mean, about us losing the Teleporter?"

Lorraine looks at me pensively. "Oh no, I guess not." She bites her lip. "I think it all worked out for the best. Mr. and Mrs. Hazelton are back together. Our grounding's off. And Eugene and Artmas are back in their homeland!"

"You're right, Lorraine." I go over to her bed to sit down beside her. "Things *did* work out for the best."

Finally, Lorraine smiles. She looks down at the photo in my hand, then smiles a little wider.

"Yes, they did," she says, then pauses for a moment. "Hey, why don't we go to the kitchen and see if we can talk Mom into letting us go to the lake for the weekend?"

"Now that's my kind of adventure!" I say.

TO BE CONTINUED...

ACKNOWLEDGMENTS

The first chapters of *Hunter Thomas and the Smelly Old Shoe* were penned when I was twelve years old. Needless to say, the book underwent a long road to completion. Without the assistance of friends, family, and co-workers, *Hunter Thomas* likely never would have been completed!

First, I would like to thank friends and family members who were the book's first readers: my parents, my grandparents Gode and Bobby Roth, my grandmother Veronica Soyars, David McCroskey, Stu Houk, and many others! Several of you provided constructive criticism that helped the book shine.

My thanks to the Barnes and Noble staff who assisted in the book's production and distribution. I'd especially like to acknowledge Victor Rios and my editor Emily Coleman, who always offered the best advice!

I'd also like to thank my teacher and fellow students in the Spring 2013 Children's Book Writing course at Gotham Writer's Workshop. Everyone offered excellent advice, and I hope you all succeed with your own artistic endeavors!

Last but not least, I would like to thank my illustrator and designer, Caroline Hadilaksono, for providing such wonderful artwork to help my story come alive!

READ ON FOR AN EXCERPT FROM
BOOK TWO IN THE SERIES:

HUNTER THOMAS

AND THE
TRIAL OF INTRIGUE

Now that Eugene and Artmas have returned to Igarthia with the Teleporter in hand, Hunter Thomas hopes that life can get back to normal. But then a mysterious invitation arrives in the mail. An invitation for Hunter, Lorraine, and the Hazeltons to travel to Igarthia...if they are willing to take the risk!

CHAPTER THREE

A COZY THOMAS DINNER

A few hours later, I'm sitting in my room thinking. Lorraine *has* found the Hazelton's invitation to Igarthia, which apparently Mr. Hazelton had thrown into the kitchen trash. It's currently sitting on Lorraine's desk, a little crumbled, with a ketchup stain on the back. Lorraine's decided that we'll go back their house tomorrow (preferably when Mr. Hazelton's *not* there) to talk to Mrs. Hazelton.

Getting up, I go to my window and look into the Hazelton's house. The lights are on and I wonder what they're doing over there. I sigh deeply. I'm still feeling pretty proud of myself about my performance this afternoon. Now I can only wait and see if I'll be able to keep up my new bravado. Just then, there's a knock on my door and Mom peeks her head in.

"Dinner, Hunter! Come on before it gets cold."

I go into the kitchen, my thoughts still half on the Hazeltons. But I'm aware enough of my surroundings to throw a glance over at Dad, who's sitting hunched over at the head of the table. Dad had come home a few hours ago very grumpy after a bad day at work, so I decide to be on my best behavior for suppertime. Sitting down, I look at Lorraine and hope she has made the same decision. But she catches my eye and winks at me in a giggly manner. I roll my eyes and try to ignore her.

Tonight, Mom's made baked chicken and broccoli. The dinner passes for a few minutes in blissful silence. But I'm reaching for another chicken leg when Dad barks suddenly, "What's so funny?"

I look up, startled. Dad's glaring at Lorraine, who's biting her lip very hard, trying to look innocent.

"Nothing, Daddy."

"What were you smiling at, then?"

"Nothing, Daddy. I was just thinking about something I read."

This might have caused everything to pass over, but then Lorraine ruins it by looking over at *me*. I fight the urge to groan.

"So what now, you've got some joke with Lorraine, do you, Hunter?" Dad says nastily.

I strive to keep my face solemn and innocent. "No, sir. I don't have a joke, sir."

"*Alright*, then," Dad says, turning back to his plate and spearing a piece of broccoli with his fork. "No more smiling."

My mother clears her throat. "Would you like some more broccoli, Daniel?"

"No, I don't want some more broccoli. You see I've got some on my plate, don't you?" Dad snaps.

"Ahem. Yes, so you do."

I sigh and push my chicken bones around on my plate. *Another cozy Thomas family dinner*, I think to myself. Maybe it *would* be nice to get out of here and go to Igarthia. I wait a few more moments before asking myself to be excused, then go down the hall to Lorraine's room. I turn on the lights and go over to her nightstand to pick up the Hazelton's invitation. Sitting down on her bed, I stare at it. Suddenly, I feel very depressed. I wish I was like Lorraine, naturally adventurous and never afraid of anything. Never having to put on an act or pretend. It would be so much easier. But just as I'm thinking these thoughts, Lorraine comes into the room.

"Oh hi, Hunter," she says, going over to the bed.

"Hi," I say. Then, before I can even think about it, I say, "Let's go over to the Hazelton's and tell them now. Let's not wait till tomorrow."

"Really?" Lorraine looks at me in surprise. "It's kind of late, isn't it?"

"It's only seven!"

"Okay, then." She grins. "Let's go. Where should we tell Mom and Daddy we're going? Out for a walk?"

I stand up. "Who cares? Let's just go."

As Lorraine and I step out the front door, Lorraine calls over her shoulder, "We're going for a walk!"

As soon as we step outside, I start to cut across our lawn to the Hazelton's door. But then I realize Lorraine's not following me. I look around, then notice her moseying down the sidewalk ten feet away.

"Lorraine, where are you going?" I call in exasperation. "I thought we were going to the Hazelton's!"

Lorraine glares at me, still walking along. "We are! We told Mom and Daddy we were going on a walk, remember?"

"So what?"

"So, they could be watching from the window!"

I groan aloud. "They're not watching from the window! Come over here!"

"Oh, alright," Lorraine huffs, prancing over to me. I shake my head, trying to ignore her idiocy. Together, we both go up the Hazelton's front porch and ring the doorbell. Mrs. Hazelton opens the door, looking at us in surprised pleasure. "Hunter, Lorraine!"

"Hi, Mrs. Hazelton," I say.

"May we come in, Mrs. Hazelton?" Lorraine asks.

"Oh, of course."

Mrs. Hazelton leads us back into the den, where Mr. Hazelton is slumped on the couch, watching TV.

"Marty, Hunter and Lorraine are here!"

"What?" Mr. Hazelton pushes himself up and stares at us.

"Sit down, children. Make room, Marty."

Marty scowls, but scoots over so Lorraine and I can sit down on the couch with him. I feel uneasy sitting in such close proximity to Mr. Hazelton, but try to look normal.

"It's so nice for you to visit again," Esther says, beaming at us. "Can I get you something to eat?"

"Um, no thank you, Mrs. Hazelton," Lorraine answers. "Actually, we have something to give you."

Then she reaches very deliberately into her pocket to take out the invitation. I have the sudden urge to grab her arm. I'm not sure so how safe it is to show Esther the invitation with Mr. Hazelton sitting right next to us, but there's nothing I can do about it now.

"It's *your* invitation to Igarthia, Mrs. Hazelton!" Lorraine exclaims, handing it to her.

Mrs. Hazelton stares at it in wonderment. "Oh, how—"

"How did you brats get that?" Mr. Hazelton snarls suddenly, getting up off the couch to glare at us.

Mrs. Hazelton stares at him in shock. "Marty, what did you call the children?"

Marty ignores her question. "Can I talk to you a minute alone, Esther? In the bedroom."

"Um, okay," Mrs. Hazelton says confusedly. They both leave the den together and I hear a door slam down the hallway.

I look at Lorraine and she looks at me.

"Do you think this is a good sign or a bad sign?" she asks.

"Probably a bad sign," I answer.

Suddenly, Lorraine gets up. "Come on."

"Where are we going?"

Lorraine rolls her eyes. "To eavesdrop! What else?"

The old Hunter probably would have made some whiny excuse about getting caught, but the *new* Hunter stands up boldly and follows her down the hallway to the Hazelton's door. Then we both get down on our stomachs on the plush carpeting to listen through the door crack. As I press my ear against the wood, I can hear Mr. Hazelton's voice saying, "—Don't know if it's a good idea, Esther."

"Marty, how could it not be a good idea?"

"It just looks suspicious is all. Why's their government inviting us over there, anyway? What do they want from us?"

"They don't want anything, they just—"

"And what about those men? Remember them? They were practically criminals!"

"Oh, why must you be so biased, Martin? You are treating two men like they are a representation of a whole country! Do you know who *else* does that? Racists."

"Oh, for God's sake!" I imagine Marty throwing up his hands in frustration. "I am *not* a racist!"

"Well, here's your chance to prove it, then."

There's silence in the bedroom. Apparently Marty is thinking hard. Then he says finally, in a weary voice, "Alright. Alright. You *can* send them your reply. See what they say. But mind you, we still *might* not go. I haven't decided for sure yet."

"Oh, Marty, thank you!" Mrs. Hazelton cries. "Thank you!"

Suddenly, there's the sound of hurried footsteps. Both Lorraine and I scramble to our feet. The door swings open and Mrs. Hazelton stands before us, beaming. "Children, we're going to Igarthia!"